"It won't work,"

he shouted. Embarrassed by his own outburst, Charlie spread his big hands, palms upward, and examined his calluses. "The men won't go for it. You're a potential source of trouble. On my trips, everyone has to pull his own weight and pitch in."

"I can certainly do that," she said flatly. "I take excellent care of myself, and I'm neither weak nor frail, as you've noticed. I happen to be able to hike twenty miles with a full backpack anytime or anyplace." Andromeda surveyed him with disdain. "I've worked geologic surveys for oil companies, and I'm teaching part-time at Pacific Polytechnic Institute. You're a bad businessman and a chauvinist if you think a little hostility and a pathetic show of male menace will discourage me."

Dear Reader,

Welcome to Silhouette! Our goal is to give you hours of unbeatable reading pleasure, and we hope you'll enjoy each month's six new Silhouette Desires. These sensual, provocative love stories are both believable and compelling—sometimes they're poignant, sometimes humorous, but always enjoyable.

Indulge yourself. Experience all the passion and excitement of falling in love along with our heroine as she meets the irresistible man of her dreams and together they overcome all obstacles in the path to a happy ending.

If this is your first Desire, I hope it'll be the first of many. If you're already a Silhouette Desire reader, thanks for your support! Look for some of your favorite authors in the coming months: Stephanie James, Diana Palmer, Dixie Browning, Ann Major and Doreen Owens Malek, to name just a few.

Happy reading!

Isabel Swift
Senior Editor

SDRL-7/85

ANN HURLEY
Catching a Comet

Silhouette Desire

Published by Silhouette Books New York

America's Publisher of Contemporary Romance

SILHOUETTE BOOKS
300 East 42nd St., New York, N.Y. 10017

ISBN: 0-373-05288-X

First Silhouette Books printing June 1986

America's Publisher of Contemporary Romance

Printed in the U.S.A.

Books by Ann Hurley

Silhouette Special Edition

Touch of Greatness #98
Hearts in Exile #167

Silhouette Desire

Chasing the Rainbow #181
Year of the Poet #233
Catching a Comet #288

Silhouette Romance

The Highest Tower #408

ANN HURLEY

sprang from a family chock-full of lawyers, teachers and scientists. After a long stint teaching literature and creative writing, Ann realized that she wanted to *write* most of all. Although she has traveled extensively, she chose to settle in Albuquerque, New Mexico, where she frequently walks across the mesa west of the city for a glimpse of the Sandias and the majestic Rio Grande.

For Roz, who gets me going,
and LaVonne, who keeps me at it.

One

Charlie saw a tall blonde through his dusty storefront window. There was a lot of her to see with the San Diego sunlight streaming through her cotton dress, and Charlie sent up silent thanks to Mother Nature for the blessings of the sun and women.

"I think I love you," he murmured into the phone he was cradling.

At the other end, Juan Robles in Tijuana, Mexico, expressed his disbelief. Charlie hastily assured him that he hadn't meant his camping supplier in the border town.

"I'll call you again, Juanito. Tomorrow, yeah. I want to hear that my equipment and food is assembled." He scratched meditatively at his brown beard, left full and glorious from his last trip, and watched the blonde open his door. "No, I'll tell you all the gory details, including the crocodiles, later. Right! Someone is here. *Bueno*, bye."

The spring breeze must have taken down his hand-printed sign. Every morning Charlie scribbled something to warn the lovely models who used to call at Dreger's Agency that their ticket to fame and fortune had been punched. Dreger had skipped out on the rent, on his bevy of beauties, and had headed for points unknown.

The blonde walked in, shading her eyes with one hand, and stopped in the doorway. Charlie's office was still unfinished, very nearly a total disaster area. Travel posters littered the floor along with all his haphazard stacks of files and papers.

"Honey," Charlie said as nicely as he could, "he isn't here. He moved. I put up a sign. The wind must have blown it down."

The sign wouldn't have done any good, anyway, he thought.

Daily, the modeling dollies arrived, portfolio and makeup bag in hand, to drive Charlie nuts. First, because they were great looking and thoroughly distracting from his business. Second, because most of them, he suspected, were as brain-dead as they were beautiful. He realized it was an unreasonable male prejudice of his but it seemed true: beauty was in direct proportion to low IQ. This blonde, from her looks alone, was undoubtedly an illiterate. A sign would have done no good.

"This is Wilde 'N Free Tours?" she asked in a marvelous clear voice. Her sandal-clad foot pushed at a leaning tower of papers and she smiled faintly at Charlie and his messy domain. "Yes, this must be the place. It looks like your safari got caught in the tail end of hurricane season."

Charlie saluted the taste of the former tenant in absentia. This Dreger guy knew how to pick them. His visitor this morning appeared to be all legs from the neck down, a vision of radiant health, and the light made her smooth straight hair a river of white gold. Gorgeous was an accurate summary, almost an understatement.

"I send everyone who comes here to the Better Business Bureau to report him," Charlie explained as he rose from behind his desk. "He took some pretty hefty fees, I gather. I hope he didn't burn you too badly, honey."

It took agility and litheness to scoot around in the room, but Charlie had those abilities, despite his size. He could push his six-foot-two frame through narrow cave openings and shinny his two hundred pounds up sheer rock faces like a prong-horned goat.

"I'm looking for Wilde 'N Free," she repeated slowly, as if he were simpleminded.

He was too far gone in admiration to care about her tone, but the message sunk in. He came closer, stepping over his debris, and stuck out his hand. She belonged here about as much as he belonged at the opening of the Debutante Ball, but who cared?

"Charles Wilde, at your service. Owner, operator, guide and chief cook and bottle washer for Wilde 'N Free Tours. I guess you're here about the African photo safari ad."

"Not at all." She shook her head, and the golden hair swung like a curtain.

He liked her rangy figure best of all, he decided. She had a nice chest but it was secondary to the overall effect of her height and slender grace. She must be close to six feet, he estimated, trying not to grin like an idiot.

"Sit down, please." He swept another set of papers off a rattan chair and pointed to it. "Of course not. Rhinos bathing in pools isn't your speed. You look more like a skier to me. How about my Chilean trip later this year?"

She looked suspiciously down at the chair and kept standing. Her eyes flicked from Charlie's face to the few leftover black-and-white photos of Dreger's star models to the cobwebs hanging in small festoons from the light fixtures. "You don't inspire me with confidence, Mr. Wilde. I sure hope your tours are better planned and organized. In fact, I'm counting on it. I'm here about—"

Charlie had to interrupt. "I know it's a mess but I was out in the Caymans for three weeks. Got back late last month and haven't had time to fix this place up. Now, lady..."

She flashed him a full dazzling smile that made him forget what he was going to say next and she sat down, crossing her remarkably long and muscular legs. Charlie had his best and worst moment of the day so far simultaneously. He wasn't sure how he knew it, but he felt this woman was trouble.

"'Lady' is a little better than 'honey,' I suppose," she said. "Wednesday, you have a Baja Peninsula trip beginning. I needed—"

He cut her off again. "That's a wilderness trek and an all-male trip. I don't know where you would have heard about it. I advertised in men's magazines like *Rod and Gun*."

"And Pacific Polytechnic's newspaper," she added. "It is not an all-male trip. You have one Andy Pruitt booked, don't you?"

His mahogany eyes met her periwinkle blue ones and narrowed. He was silent, sizing up the situation, wondering what he had done to deserve this. "Don't tell me," Charlie said finally.

"Yes," she said. "Meet Andromeda Pruitt. I have my confirmation and a canceled check for my five hundred dollar deposit on a Baja Wilderness trip." She opened her purse and took out a few folded sheets of paper and a pair of blue-rimmed glasses.

"I have a problem," said Charlie. "The ad clearly indicated—"

"I don't give a diddely-damn what your intent was," Ms. Pruitt said, peering at him through her glasses. Her eyes looked enormous, spectacular. "The Civil Rights Amendment prohibits—"

"Oh don't give me any of that tired stuff," barked Charlie. He paced up and down as best he could in the cramped space in front of her. "The peninsula is a rough place. This is a long, nasty trip over some of the worst roads in the Northern Hemisphere. The Baja is no place for a woman."

It was the wrong tack to take with her. Usually honesty was the best policy but she bristled, visibly.

"I'm here and qualified to go."

"No," he insisted with a shake of his too long hair. "No, honey, you are not. I am talking about the real world, Andy Pruitt. I thought I had five men signed up for a get-away-from-it-all trip. There will be four men and myself going Wednesday, it appears. Not four men, me and one lady. I can just see that. A cozy group for a jaunt, pup-tenting in the middle of nowhere with someone who looks like you."

"What does that mean?" Andromeda snapped. "I am sure my looks have a good deal less to do with this than a certain narrow mind-set. Your opinion wouldn't stand up in a court of law." She held out his confirmation and was ignored.

"It won't wash with the other men," Charlie countered, "or me. You aren't going."

She glared back. "Hold it right there. I signed up for what's *my* best chance to view Halley's Comet from an unpolluted southerly site. We are talking here about my vacation and my hobby. I am signed, sealed and delivered. This trip is my dream, Charles Wilde 'N Free. You can't spoil it for me."

Charlie sighed heavily. "Yeah, I should have guessed it would be something wiggy like a comet with you.

Hon . . . Ms. Pruitt, there are several excellent special tours and fancy cruises being run with other agencies for the express purpose of star-watching or comet-seeking or whatever you are into. My tour isn't.

"There isn't much sense in a woman wanting to go with a bunch of sportsmen who are set on exploring, fishing, swapping lies and drinking beer away from their wives and girlfriends."

"A month of clean skies and undisturbed nights made sense to me," she retorted. "It is worth some struggle, too, and most of my savings."

"This is not a scientific expedition," he growled. "It is about adventure, a masculine desire for freedom."

"Sorry to mess up your plans," Andromeda said without sincerity. "I wasn't going to make any scientific discoveries. Halley's is the best known and most studied of the regular cometary visitors to our solar system. But it is a once in a lifetime experience to see it. I missed it in 1910. I won't miss it on this swing around the sun."

"Miss Pruitt . . ."

"Ms." She hissed the "z" sound like a reptile at him.

Charlie rolled his eyes upward and clasped his hands firmly behind his back. He loved women. He had loved quite a few and had even married one. He would never, ever strike one, but this creature was annoying him.

"Ms. Pruitt," he exhaled slowly, "maybe you didn't completely understand the nature of the Baja wilderness. The peninsula *is* attached to Southern California, but it is Mexico and it is a big, dangerous place, largely uninhabited."

At least she gave him her attention. Charlie waxed eloquent, but avoided looking at her directly because she was really very distracting. He was self-conscious about her open appraisal of him as he walked and talked, aware that he did have a good physique, and women weren't generally averse to his features. Did she like what she saw?

"The Baja is underdeveloped. Things haven't changed since the beginning of time and there aren't many cities worth the name. It has desert and mountain and ocean and rutted roads so deep you could lose a car in them."

She nodded and folded her hands.

"We won't stick to the new two-lane blacktop that runs to La Paz," he said, feeling he was making headway. "We want to travel a thousand road miles through country where we can camp and see the land . . ."

"Or spot a comet," she finished. "I know most of that stuff and I intend to go."

"It won't work!" he shouted. Embarrassed by his own outburst, Charlie spread his big hands, palms upward, and examined his own calluses. "The men won't go for it. You are a potential source of trouble. On my trips, everyone has to pull his own weight and pitch in."

"I certainly can do that," she said flatly. "I take excellent care of myself and I am neither weak nor frail, as you have noticed. I happen to be able to hike twenty miles with a full backpack any time or any place."

He tried a different technique, stopping in his tracks to loom over her and stare down. He drew his heavy eyebrows together and made his mouth tight, firm. "I'll refund your check. I'll give you the names and numbers of those other agencies."

"Their prices are exorbitant and I have limited funds. You can rest assured I did some careful research. I am not a sloppy person like others I could name, Mr. Wilde." She surveyed the office once more with disdain. "I've worked geological surveys for oil companies and I'm teaching part-time at Pacific Polytechnic Institute. You're a bad businessman and a chauvinist if you think a little hostility and a pathetic show of male menace will discourage me. Oh, Bob Carver of Waverly Oil recommended you. I forgot to mention it while you were lecturing."

Charlie went back to his desk and sat down hurriedly. He plastered a kindlier expression on his face and made his voice softer, silkier. He disliked this woman. He could learn to hate her, no matter how fine looking she was. He wished he could look a trifle pathetic but that was impossible, he knew.

"I can understand your disappointment," he said. "I'm sure we can work this out. You appear to be a reasonable, intelligent and perceptive woman. However there are no facilities on my tour for a woman. I have connections in this business and I might manage to get you on the Maelstrom cruise—for the same price we agreed on, of course. You'd be happy with that arrangement, wouldn't you?"

"I'd be a fool not to be," laughed Andromeda. "Their cheapest cabin was twice your price, and I'm hardly the luxury cruise type."

She smoothed out a wrinkle in the skirt of her spotless white-and-blue dress. Charlie couldn't imagine her scrabbling through the sand and dust and snakes of the Mexican wilderness.

He relaxed and smiled. "Whether it's comets or moons you're after, I'll help. It's in the bag. It'll take a few phone calls and some friendly trade talk but I'll get right on it. How about dinner tonight? We'll meet, eat and I'll tell you what's available."

"Let me establish firmly in your mind that I'm not a fool," she said with another winning smile. "I am not available, Charles Wilde, if that's what you were thinking. I won't be headed off at the pass about this trip and I'm not looking for romance, just a comet."

"You see one comet, you've seen them all," muttered Charlie under his breath. He waved his fingers at her as if making a pass was the furthest thing from his mind. "I'm trying to be nice. We can part on good terms; that's good business. You might want to go to Africa someday, right?"

She bent down, picked up a scrap of paper from the floor and wrote on it, eyeing him all the time. "Here's my phone number. I might trust you to scale the Himalayas with, but I'm dubious about your reliability across a dinner table. You are a bit of a wolf, aren't you?"

He denied it emphatically. "I am taking a bunch of guys down the dusty trail south, not dancing you down the primrose path, Andromeda Pruitt."

She laughed, a nice, full laugh, the kind he really liked. Sexy. Throaty.

"Andy," she corrected. "You have the Good Scout act down pat, Charlie. You can call me later. This does not have to turn into the Geneva Salt Talks, and you aren't required to lay on the charm with a trowel."

The piece of paper was still clutched in her hand, and he thought she might be swayed further. "Dinner at the White Rose. Their seafood is terrific. We'll have this all straightened out. This is going to be a tough assignment, you know. I've promised I will switch you to a trip you'll like and can live with, financially. I may have to pull strings . . ."

"Anything to go," she said sweetly and stood up. "Halley's Comet will not be around again until 2061 and I don't expect to be. It's now or never for Pruitt. Eight o'clock?" She added another line on her note.

He shook hands eagerly and held hers too long, waiting for the address. He squeezed her fingers firmly, but she didn't wince, pull away or extend the paper. They stood there together just clasping hands, fingers linked and eyes locked.

"One more thing about me," she continued. "I don't give up. I have been looking forward to a vacation for a year and to the comet for longer than that. I'm going to see it. I don't give up."

"I can believe that," Charlie said softly. He wondered fleetingly if anyone would believe she was an astronomer. He wondered what it would be like to kiss an astronomer. "I'll help every way I can. I really am a Good Scout."

She gave him the slip of paper and turned to leave. Stepping over a stack of files, she looked back over her shoulder and grinned, obviously dubious. "Perhaps," she said. "I'd like to know what your merit badges were in though."

Five minutes after she was gone, Charlie realized he was still grinning. The last sight of her—those supple, lovely curves, and her hair swaying like a little wave to match the sway of her hips—was still clear in his mind. He liked hazards and he appreciated the natural wonders of the world; Andromeda Pruitt seemed to be both.

Andy waited outside her building. She wasn't going to compound the error she had already made by allowing Mr. Wilde into her apartment. Accepting his dinner invitation mystified her. Why had she done it?

All right, she liked the way he looked but she didn't care much for him. Her first impression of the man was the one she should have gone by. He was somewhat fierce, a grizzled and attractive animal. His eyes warned not to fool with him. His wide, mobile mouth expressed things he didn't say. Above all, he was a macho male with a primitive mentality in a well-muscled carcass.

The man was incapable of diplomacy or tact. The implications for tonight's get-together weren't even handled subtly. She knew, without question, what the message behind the meal was. Sweet talk and other sweet things were on Charlie Wilde's menu. So why was she standing here?

A bright red Jeep with roll bars turned the corner. Andy waggled her fingers at the driver.

"You are punctual," she said with a nod, climbing in unassisted. "Maybe that virtue makes up for the messiness."

Charlie Wilde showed her his teeth, white and even and large. "You are a knockout. I really like the dress."

She glanced down at the black shirtwaist printed with shooting stars. It was one of her few decent outfits purchased to teach in. "Thank you. It's nothing special."

"You wear it well," Charlie said, "and it is a stargazer's vision, to boot. I still can't quite see you as an oil field expert or an astronomer. Are you, really?"

She had to pluck a few wayward strands of blond hair out of her mouth before she answered. The breeze was whipping her hair all around her face, and Charlie Wilde seemed to enjoy seeing her getting windblown. She didn't mind— either the wind or his enjoyment.

"Unless this is just a silly attempt to make conversation, I'll tell you," Andy said quietly. "I'm a very, very good amateur astronomer. I have several published articles and I shared the honors a few years ago with a Japanese hobbyist for discovering a new comet."

When Charlie had been talking about the Baja, he tried to make it sound awful and scary, but his own enthusiasm for such places had peeked through. When Andy started talking about her passion for the skies, the same thing happened. She heard herself take off and tell him all about the Sabusawa-Pruitt Comet, the registry of comets and the importance of amateurs in discovery and tracking of these strange cosmic wanderers.

"So, with few professionals able to devote time or energy to comets and even fewer who would if they could, it is pretty much up to people like me, night owls with telescopes and an incurable lust for these space snowballs."

She had run out of breath and words. The man next to her was smiling but in a nice way, not laughing at her unusual fascination and short lecture on comets. She had to laugh, too, guessing how she looked and what she sounded like.

It wasn't necessary to go so far as revising her original opinion of Charlie Wilde, but Andy did note how nice his eyes were. He had sparkling, smiling brown eyes. They weren't nearly as tough and uncompromising tonight. He wasn't, either. He looked downright intelligent and interested.

After today's initial encounter, Andy wouldn't have supposed they would have much to talk about. Somehow she had been mistaken. All the way to the restaurant, while they waited for their table, and even as they sat down, their conversation never stopped or faltered.

Charlie had left college to take up a casual friend's offer to travel with him and had never gone back. He had been places Andy could only vaguely visualize on her mental atlas. He'd done the most peculiar things and brought back the wildest assortment of souvenirs and mementos. He had a good, thriving business and that fact was sheer accident. It was also an accident, as far as she was concerned, that he was still alive, from some of the harrowing stories he told her.

"And people think I'm peculiar," she exclaimed softly, peering across the candles and flower arrangement at him. "Wow! I keep funny hours off in the night alone and I've traveled all over the western states with survey crews. But I never explored the Amazon Basin with two folks who didn't speak the same language as I did."

"It was fun," he laughed. "Exciting. Unprofitable but worth every second. I'm the original Good Time Charlie, I guess."

"So I suspected," Andy muttered, studying her menu. She blinked at the prices in the right-hand margin. What a strange man! He was operating a business more for pleasure than profit and taking someone he scarcely knew to one of San Diego's classiest and most expensive restaurants.

After they ordered, Andy decided she'd like to delve a little deeper into Charlie Wilde, the man. She wanted to know more about this person she was anticipating spending several weeks with. Surprises spotted through the eyepiece of her telescope were welcome but she would rather not be surprised by this man any more than she'd already been.

"I can see you kayaking, and loving it," she said. "I can understand why you climb mountains every chance you get, but this atmosphere—" she swept her hand around the sumptuous surroundings "—doesn't jibe with your image. What was the idea of taking me here? To impress me?"

"To soften the blow, or seal a deal," Charlie answered without hesitation. He fiddled with the knot of his tie as if he were going to take it off and return to the open-shirted explorer she'd met earlier. "If I could deliver on my promise, I wanted to celebrate. My ex-wife always loved this overpriced oyster bar and dragged me here on every flimsy excuse of an occasion. If my wheeling and dealing fell through, I wanted you to be in a good mood."

"Well, which is it?" asked Andy. His blunt honesty impressed her. She repeated her question and still got no answer, just a tipping of more white wine into her glass. Raising the crystal goblet to her lips, Andy saw a flash of rainbows fall on her hand and the linen cloth and suspected why he was hesitating. "That bad, huh?"

"Six hundred dollars more and you'll be on the North Star with a reserved deck chair, staring up at a comet."

"Same price, you said. The Maelstrom, you said. The North Star will be mobbed with society types, not scholars."

"Can't be done." Charlie was staring intently at her.

"No." She took another sip of wine, a hummingbird swallow. "Tell me what time the group is gathering in Tijuana. I'll be ready."

"I'll pay the difference if I have to," groaned Charlie. "What's a few hundred bucks? Andy, it's a fabulous deal. The Star cruise ships have unbelievable food..."

"It's the principle, as well as the payment. I signed aboard your ship, not theirs. Six hundred is not chicken feed. I hate caviar. If I had six thousand I could have gone to the Andes, the best place for observation."

"You're stubborn," he said, setting his hand down too hard and making the carnations jiggle. "I wouldn't have done all that smooth talking and wheedling if I'd known you were such an irritating, irrational woman. The cruise tickets are going for three times what you'd be paying—"

"I'm going," Andy said, interrupting him. "I make my own plans and pay my own way. I've been supporting myself since I was seventeen. I was willing to compromise if it didn't cost me in time, trouble or money."

"Big compromise!" His deep, booming voice was attracting a lot of attention from other diners. "Boy, oh, boy, try to treat women like regular people and see where it gets you. Try to reason with them... Just try. You can't go with me. The others would pull out of the trip and that would be a bust for them and a financial disaster for me."

He was on the edge of raving. Andy leaned back into the damasked chair and watched, fascinated. She dealt with men who thought her an oddball and a loner. They were, generally, quiet, soft-spoken, conservative men. They were either earth scientists, professional scholars or oil company businessmen. In her whole life, she had never met anyone like Charlie Wilde.

"This is a one-man operation, start to finish. I'm the chief. What I say, goes—and you don't. I'll lose my reputation, my clients, my miserable profits..."

"These other men... they might be more agreeable than you are," Andy interjected when Charlie had to pause for breath. "I'll speak to them myself."

The waiter stood there, mesmerized, and was obviously debating whether or not to put their meals before them. Andy smiled at him and nodded, supposing that a full mouth might slow Charlie down. Charlie menaced the waiter and slouched forward, covering the space in front of him so the plates couldn't be deposited.

"I won't take you," he declared. "Some of the gents would be all too happy, I'm sure, if you tagged along, but I wouldn't. And I'll tell you why."

"I'm starved," Andy said. She made the waiter put both dinners on her side of the table.

"I'd have to stand guard over you every night," ranted Charlie, snatching Andy's fork from her hand. "Maybe you don't look in the mirror much, honey, but they've all got eyes. Someone is bound to get more wild and free than you bargained for...."

Andromeda grabbed a teaspoon and dug into her steaming casserole dish. "I'm petrified," she managed to say. "Do you know that in 1910, an Oklahoma sheriff had to save a virgin from being sacrificed by superstitious folks afraid of Halley's?"

The head waiter bustled up, all shiny black efficiency and service in his tuxedo. "Is there, perhaps, a problem here, sir? Madam?"

"This woman is a problem," shouted Charlie. "I'm not feeding anyone who is bent on ruining me."

"His snapper is a little dry," Andy commented, tasting a morsel. "Could we have a little bit of drawn butter on the side?"

"Certainly." The head waiter gulped and looked around nervously. "Do you think you might keep this discussion somewhat more subdued?" He was pleading with Andy, avoiding any indication that he noticed Charles Wilde.

"I make it a practice to let everyone be himself," Andy replied. "I don't concern myself with how other people judge me. I usually extend the same courtesy to others. My companion is loud but harmless."

Charlie closed his jaw with a loud snap and made a rude noise in his throat. The head waiter sailed off, satisfied.

"You don't just study outer space," he said in a subdued but angry tone. "You should have told me that you were *from* outer space. You don't get shook easily. You do whatever you want. You don't give a damn what I think of you."

"Just like you," said Andy with a wide smile. "And when it comes to stubborn, irrational and irritating, Wilde, you could match me any day. We'll have a great time in Mexico."

He lowered his bearded jaw, thought better of it, and licked his lower lip before closing his mouth. She felt she had made tremendous progress in getting to know him.

She had learned something else, too. His outburst over, Charlie resumed the conversation and dinner as if nothing had happened. He didn't sulk or scowl or grump at her through the rest of the meal. His argument had genuinely been to put across his point of view, not to push her around. Andy liked that. In fact, she was willing to admit to herself that despite his unusual qualities—or because of them—she liked Charles Wilde. Sort of.

As they got up to leave, Charlie sighed deeply and reached for Andy's arm. It was the first time all night she'd had physical contact with him and she liked the firm but gentle grip he took on her. He kept his hand on her all the way out to the parking lot and paused, still holding her, at the passenger side of his Jeep.

"No matter what happens, this is going to be interesting," he said, staring directly into her eyes. "You can pitch the men in Tijuana and I'll abide by what they decide. I won't like it if you go but I'll live with it. I don't think it's going to happen, personally, so I'm not worried."

She was aware of his body heat, the scent of a starched shirt, a piny soap. There was no artificial sweetness of cologne to Charlie; it would have shocked her if there was.

"Big compromise," Andy mimicked his own words. "You'll go halfway if there's no danger that they'll take me."

"I don't do anything halfway," Charlie said.

He put his arms around her without warning and pulled her into his territory. The kiss he gave her made tiny flashes of light dance behind her closed eyelids. No, there wasn't anything halfway about Charlie Wilde or the way he kissed her.

His lips found hers and stayed there, catching Andy off guard and unprepared. He didn't mince words and he didn't skimp on kisses. For such a rough-looking man, his mouth was surprisingly tender, warm and gently damp. Andy found out that he tasted fresh and inviting and that his beard didn't tickle much.

She could have found out more but he tipped slightly back and regarded her quietly for a minute.

"It's kind of a shame you won't be going," Charlie whispered. "I'd like a few more of those. You are a pretty spectacular lady, Andromeda Pruitt. I've never met anyone quite like you."

"I'm going," she repeated, "and not to fool around. But you could kiss me again, Charlie. We haven't crossed the border yet."

Two

Evidently, when it came to kisses—but not trips—Charlie was happy to comply with Andy's every wish. This time, she was ready when he delivered the second kiss. She put as much into it as he did, enjoying the feeling of his big frame next to hers and the sensations he inspired. He wasn't enthusiastic about her as a companion, but Charlie really appreciated her as a woman and made no secret of it.

"I'll take you home," he said huskily. There was a pause before he unwound his arms. "I don't do my best work in parking lots."

Andy got into the Jeep, smiling to herself. "I don't, either. I wouldn't call what just happened 'work,' however. In case you have further plans for tonight, I should tell you that it's quitting time. You are satisfying your curiosity about me and vice versa. That's all."

The roar of the engine starting up covered his retort, but she caught his expression of disappointment and surprise before it faded. "Aren't you going to ask me in?" he repeated as they sped down the boulevard. "We seem to be getting along so well."

She just laughed and watched the city whip by. Whatever this evening was set up to prove, she held on to some new discoveries about Charlie and herself for closer examination later. His animal magnetism, if that's what it was, was strong and compelling. He couldn't talk her into doing anything she didn't want to do, but he distinctly had the power to make her want more of him. Charlie might be right about this trip having its share of dangers.

"Thanks for an interesting evening," she said as the apartment came into sight. She waited until he flicked off the ignition key and turned expectantly toward her, and offered him her hand, not her cheek or her mouth. "You better give me the particulars about Wednesday right now. I'm all out of instant coffee, so we'll call it a night here."

"Weird," pronounced Charlie loudly. "I'll only be gone a month, Andy. Even if you don't go, I'd call you when I got back. I think we might be good together. You fight like a cornered tiger and kiss me like someone out of a fever dream, then brush me off. What's this all about? Do you want me to slink off into the night, rejected, or to make love to you?"

"I want you to live up to your promise," answered Andy. She thought it unwise to comment on the amazing promise of their kisses. "Your reputation and your own advertising proclaim how travel with Wilde is an out-of-this-world adventure, a memory for a lifetime. Well, deliver!"

"Hotel El Presidente in Tijuana," Charlie said in a slightly weary voice. "My group meets in front at eight o'clock *en punto*. That means, 'on the dot,' Ms. Pruitt."

"I know what it means." She opened the door when he made no move to get out and act the gentleman. "Okay.

How about me catching a ride down there with you? I can be ready anytime you say.''

His eyes widened into a stare. "Wow, you have got nerve. And you ought to come equipped with a weather vane so I'd know which way the wind is blowing. Hot, cold, north, south... You took me by storm today—and especially a little while ago, Pruitt—but I'm watching my step from here on out."

"So am I," she chorused demurely and took her house keys out. "Was that a yes or no for a ride?"

He gave her a dirty look. "Take the bus or rent a car like everyone else. Unless you care to invite me in, of course, and attempt to change my best-laid plans again with some more feminine wiles."

"Not a chance," Andy whispered. "We aren't even good friends yet, much less lovers. I'll see you in Tijuana, Charlie."

"Not with any luck or if I see you first," he groaned, "but the way things are tending...."

She disappeared into the building's foyer. Through the plate glass, Andy saw him sit there, hunched slightly over the wheel and mumbling to himself.

Border towns got bad press and publicity. Tijuana, with its curio shops and bars, fast marriage and divorce parlors, was no exception. But Tijuana was also a big city with sides that the tourist trade rarely saw. The sleazy or glittery parts weren't the sum total of the town; there were fine hotels, friendly people and accommodating merchants for someone like Charles Wilde to work with. Tijuana, Mexico was the entrance to all of the Baja Peninsula.

The tour was assembling outside the Hotel Presidente. Slowly, Andy walked up the street, balancing her big suitcase, her small valise and a folding deck chair. It was fortunate the bus station was not far from the hotel.

She could see Charlie and a group of men in front of the Presidente. It seemed as if there were a million men, and most of them were charging around, loading and moving cardboard boxes into three heavy-duty, four-wheel drive vehicles. Mr. Wilde 'N Free himself was shrieking at the top of his lungs, gesturing at the caravan and wrestling with several bright red gas cans.

"Hi," said Andy, getting closer. She elbowed a bewildered onlooker aside and tapped Charlie on the shoulder. "Hi, there. Off to a flying start, I see."

"They can take a flying..." He didn't spin around until he finished berating someone thoroughly. When he did turn, Charlie gaped at the sight of her and tugged at his beard, surveying her carefully. "You sure look different."

She had fastened her hair into two plaits and there wasn't a trace of makeup on her face or a spot of polish on her nails. Her khaki shorts and white camp shirt met with his approval, and there wasn't a better pair of hiking boots on the market.

"I was serious about this trip. I told you I read up on it."

"We'll see. You don't have your bunk secure yet," he reminded her. "Damn, I can not get anyone here to find those extra cans of gas and the chamois I ordered. I'll kill Juan Robles if he—"

Andy nodded, spoke in rapid and fluent Spanish to the nearest native and then to the man he indicated. "There you go," she said to Charlie. "He'll get them and find Juan for you. Now, about my trip approval?"

"Wow!" Charlie ran his hand through his bushy, curly hair and shook his head in disbelief. "You speak Spanish, and well. Better than mine, for sure."

"I was born in Texas," Andy said as if that settled the matter. "Hey, what about meeting my companions?"

There was no reply. Charlie was concentrating on the final crates of supplies, dividing them equally and worrying aloud about the placement and weight of each one. He began to chat about how suicidal it was to leave without ten days' store of food, potable water and extra fuel. He was plainly avoiding the subject.

Andy spotted her fellow travelers. They didn't look particularly rough and tough, although Charlie did. He was wearing a blue T-shirt with the hideous face of the Aztec sun god printed in white and a disreputable pair of torn jeans. His boots, with soles two inches thick, made hers look like ballet slippers. He had a formidable knife sheathed on his belt, a tightly rolled red bandana around his forehead to hold back his hair, and there was a no-nonsense glint in his eyes.

Her assessment was confirmed when he stopped long enough to make an aside to her. "It's batty, too, to think your disguise as an overgrown Girl Scout will help your case. Andy, you are a woman. Even in a paper grocery sack, it would be discernible."

"These are my ordinary working clothes on surveys," she started to explain.

He slammed the tailgate on the last van shut and hollered to the crowd. The few men she'd spotted stepped out, dragging gun cases and canvas satchels with fishing tackle.

"The moment of truth," he said. "Guys, a few final reminders. Listen up, please! This is not a democracy. None of my trips are. I'm the one with the big veto, the deciding vote. I've been up and down the Baja four times; I know the land, the dangers, the good spots. In short, I am the boss. I can get you in and out safely with a minimum of fuss and a maximum of fun, fins and feathers."

There was a scuffling of feet, a few indistinct noises of agreement. Charlie reached into his jeans and pulled out three sets of keys, handing out the other two.

"Two of you have been with me before. George and Bill haven't," continued Charlie. "My way or no way at all, fellows. It's a helluva long walk through the peninsula."

Andy cleared her throat very audibly.

Charlie pretended she wasn't there. "We are guests in Mexico. Let's not give anyone any reason not to invite us back."

Andy brushed up against him, jostling him slightly. "Excuse me," she hissed. "Before you say, 'Start your engines,' could we...?"

"Yeah," muttered Charlie without so much as a flick of his finger toward her. "There's one more thing..."

"I am not a thing," she corrected.

"I goofed," Charlie said to the men. "I sold a spot to Andy Pruitt of Pacific Polytechnic Institute. This may be a saddle sore for some of you..."

"Don't poison the well," snapped Andromeda. "You just about have forbidden them to agree. You make yourself sound like God."

Charlie didn't even bother to introduce her around, one by one, to the members of the group. He glanced up and back at the men. "This is Andromeda Pruitt. She wants to be included in. She wants to tag along."

Andy put her deck chair against the bumper and set her suitcase down with a thump. "I paid to go," she announced loudly. "I wish to correct Mr. Wilde. He thinks it's a bad idea and won't work. I think he's full of it." There was muffled laughter from the men. "If there aren't any objections from any of you, he has agreed to live up to his bargain... which he should do."

A gray-haired man, the oldest traveler, shuffled up and tugged at the bill of his San Diego Padres baseball cap. He studied Andy for a minute.

"I'm George Polachek, retired electrical engineer." He tipped his head slightly to one side. "This was supposed to be the boys' night out, to be plain about it. Having a female with us will put a good-sized, although pretty, crimp in the plans."

"I won't be around much. You won't see much of me, Mr. Polachek," replied Andy. "I am taking a telescope, a pair of binoculars, and a superb camera to occupy my evenings. You can be whooping it up and I won't object or get in your way. I don't have to hear to watch the sky. I won't be listening to the talk around the fire."

George adjusted his cap and rubbed the bridge of his large nose thoughtfully. "Humph! That means you'll be dead tired and dead weight during the day, then."

Wilde bobbed his head up and down behind Polachek's back. Andy wanted to smack him with something, preferably a heavy blunt object, but she kept her features composed and her voice even.

"Not at all, Mr. Polachek. I've been an astronomy hobbyist for years and years. I am used to working hard and sleeping very little. I'll be functional but somewhat preoccupied during the day. You won't even know I'm there most of the time."

"Let me think about this a second," said Polachek gruffly. "I don't know..." He turned his back on her and stepped over to the others. "What do you think, Ray?"

"I think we should have left ten minutes ago," grumbled the man being addressed. "For crying out loud, I wasn't looking forward to a debate on the Equal Rights Amendment. There's doves, ducks and geese, there's marlin and sailfish waiting out there."

"Gentlemen, I appeal to you . . ."

"You certainly do," a disembodied voice answered.

Andy didn't bother to find out which of the assembled men was already her fan. "I am paid up, I'm packed. How about some fair play?"

"Who's she talking to?"

"Not you, Bud. She said 'gentlemen.'"

Another voice added, "That's plural. She appealed to more than one of us. That's true, too. Are we going to vote?"

Andy rubbed away a few beads of sweat from her upper lip and scanned them collectively. "I can speak Spanish, read palms, steer by the stars and make the best damned campfire stew you ever ate—with biscuits. What do you say?"

Charlie Wilde had folded his muscular arms across his middle and was leaning back against a vehicle. There was an amused expression on his face, bordering on a smirk. When Andy caught his eye, he shrugged slightly as if to say it was exactly what he'd warned her about. Thanks but no thanks.

"Hey, you pays your money and you takes your chances," said George Polachek. He hooked his thumb into the waistband of his pants and peered curiously at Andy. "That's the American way. If you think you can do it, little lady, you sure can try."

The phrase "little lady" made Charlie snort loudly. Andy gave him a dirty look with a fillip of triumph thrown in for good measure. One down, three to go.

Two men stepped forward. They were very clearly a father-son team; the fortyish man stood close to the younger replica of himself.

"I'm Ray Morgan," the older one introduced himself and shook hands. "And this is my boy, Mike."

Mike colored like a shy youngster. He didn't like "boy" any more than Andy liked "little lady." She shook his hand, too, and gave him an empathetic glance.

"Do you hunt or fish?" inquired the father bluntly. "This trip is for sport, y'know."

"I hunt down erratic meteors and wild comets, and fish for rare shots of the skies," said Andy. "I'm going after Halley's where the waters, so to speak, are better and clearer. I won't be any trouble. I'll stay downwind of game."

Charlie wandered over and stood at her shoulder. He couldn't resist a few low-pitched asides to her. "You should run for office, Pruitt."

Mike Morgan couldn't take his eyes off her, not even when his father nudged him to speak up. "If you can make stew, it's fine with me," he said slowly. "We went white water rafting with Charlie last year. It was strictly survival fare. Right, Dad?"

Ray Morgan looked totally disinterested. "Let's go. I don't give a hoot in hell who's along. I don't care what the food's like. I want to hunt. I want to fish."

"You're really cooking now," grumbled Charlie into her ear. He began to jingle a heavy set of keys in his hand, nervously. There was only one more participant in this play who had a vote to cast.

"Only thing is . . . she can't ride with me. She won't drive me," George objected. "I get enough of women yammering at home. I've got a wife, two daughters. Even our cat's a girl."

His partner was Bill Wiggins. Andy was relieved when she realized she would not have to contend with the most hostile and the least hostile of the men.

"All right, let's get this show on the road!" Charlie shouted. He appeared to step into his role as wagon master and head scout without any trepidation. He took Andy's forearm and steered her toward the lead vehicle—his. "Guess I'm stuck with you," he said, but he didn't sound terribly displeased.

"I can navigate," volunteered Andy. "Researchers are good at reading obscure texts. I took a peek at the maps you're using. You need a geological survey hand like me along. Where did you get them? From a passing conquistador?"

"Just about," laughed Charlie, firing up the engine and waving his hand out his window back at the Morgans. "Okay, I'll be keeping an eye on you. It's only fair that you keep your eyes on the map and the road. I want plenty of conversation, too. I don't know beans about astronomy or petroleum studies so I'll pick topics I know volumes about."

Andy put her arm on the door, winced at the heat of the metal, and gave him a suspicious glance. "What's the first subject?"

"Marriage," said Charlie with a grin.

"Marriage?" She fanned herself with her hand. "How many times were you married?"

"Once. But it was all marriages condensed into one, so I wouldn't have to repeat such a complete experience or do further research."

"Oh, it must have been a bad experience." She clucked her tongue in mock sympathy.

He beeped his horn loudly and repeatedly until a man came out of a house to chase his three goats out of the narrow roadway. "It covered the usual five stages: great, good, bad, indifferent and impossible. Jane was great when I was good, she was bad when I was indifferent, and we were finally impossible together. It was a nice place to visit, marriage, but I wouldn't . . ."

". . . want to live there," Andy finished for him. "You don't need to tell me this stuff, you know. I didn't ask."

"Look for a little switchback about four miles up, marked with a basalt boulder and a trident of saguaro, will you?" Charlie was fighting the wheel, struggling to maneuver the TravelAll into ruts and out. "No, I know you didn't ask. I thought I'd tell you and ask you a few personal questions."

"I have never been married. Or close to married," Andy said quickly. "I am twenty-eight and not inexperienced with people of your gender, however. Before you ask for references or preferences, the answer is still no."

"You speak right up for yourself, don't mince words or act coy," Charlie noted loud and clear. "I like that in you, Andromeda. You're a real lady but you aren't prissy or phony."

"Thanks," she said. "Will this rock and saguaro be easily distinguishable from the seven thousand other clumps and stones we are passing, or not?"

He took his eyes off the miserable dusty trail they were following and grinned broadly at her. "No, but if you can tell stars and oil fields apart from each other, it should be a snap for you."

She mentioned casually that she had star charts to use at night, fine reports and computer printouts from oil companies during the day. The poorest one was light-years better than Charlie's maps. "There," she shouted above the chugging of the engine. "Turn there."

She didn't have a clue whether she was right or wrong. It was going to be all chance and luck from the look of it. But Charlie spun the wheels and sent up rooster tails of dirt and pebbles, and the other two vehicles swung duly into file after them.

They traveled hours and hours at a snail's pace. Twenty-five miles an hour was like speeding. Andy checked the position of the sun once more. "I simply don't understand you," Andy said angrily. "We are not heading south. We are skirting the border, going in an approximately east-northeasterly direction.''

"Thank you,'' said Charlie dryly. He snatched the canteen away from her and dribbled water all over himself. "I am not lost, for your information. We're heading for Tecate, a very nice town. There will hardly be a tourist in sight and they have a thriving cottage industry. You'll love it. Relax, will you?''

"What industry?'' she asked suspiciously.

"Beer,'' he said with a grin and shook some water drops off his beard. "Two of Mexico's finest breweries are located there. The men will want to take on more supplies in Tecate, I'm sure.''

She curled her lip at him. "Oh, I'm sure! And when everyone is falling down silly, I'll load you all up and drive on alone, I suppose. This was billed as a natural adventure, not a bar-hopping tour.''

"You don't smoke,'' he observed. "You're going to tell me you don't drink, either. It's a lie. Remember, I took you out to dinner. You're thirsty, aren't you? It's warm and it'll get hotter when we're around the desert at Laguna Salada. Lighten up, Pruitt.''

Taking back the canteen, she sipped and screwed the top on tightly. Taking his advice, she stretched her legs out as best she could and leaned back into the upholstery. The scenery was worth watching, although not spectacularly different from California at this point. There were flowers here and there along the roadside and an occasional handsome stand of ocotillo cactus topped with bright red blooms. She pointed out some interesting rock formations to Charlie.

Until they got farther into the interior of the peninsula, she wouldn't find the right conditions for her night watches.

She might as well enjoy a couple of days of sightseeing and so resigned herself to being as gracious about it as possible.

"After this beer barrel fiesta, what?" she asked. "I'm trying to plan my own activities around yours. I need it dark and deserted for good results."

"Me, too," kidded Charlie, giving her a leer. "You better keep one eye on 'Sweet William' Wiggins by the way. The man has an active imagination. Being partnered with George will cool him out, though. That old duffer will talk his ears off and tell him about a hundred shaggy dog stories a day."

"You know some of these men pretty well," observed Andy. "They travel with you again and again so they must like and trust you."

"Do you?" he asked unexpectedly. "Like and trust me?"

"Like," she confirmed, "in a guarded sort of way. Trust? I don't know, Charlie. You seem pretty erratic, not to mention eccentric. It's a style I grew up with but haven't run into lately."

He wanted to know what she meant and Andy ended up by telling him an abridged and expurgated version of her family history. Lawton Pruitt, her father, was a name Charlie had read several times and never associated with her. The Pruitt patriarch was celebrated for his intellectual achievements in astrophysics but regarded as a social kook for his unorthodox life-style.

"He's away in the Sierra Nevadas right now," said Andy. "He took his newest Mrs. Pruitt for their honeymoon and her mountain climbing lessons about eight months ago. I haven't heard from him since but that's nothing new. He disappeared one whole year and turned up in Rhodesia."

"How old is he?" asked Charlie incredulously.

"He was born the year Halley's came around last time and the year Mark Twain died, incidentally. Nineteen ten." She smiled when Charlie whistled low and appreciatively.

"Yes, he's a pretty vigorous sort, my dad. This wife is his fourth...or is Tiffany his fourth and Bonita his fifth? Well, Lawton keeps getting married and Bonita is two years younger than I am. The main difficulty he has with women seems to be that they can't keep up with him, physically or mentally. Although Dad claims he's slowing down and entering his dotage."

"Doesn't sound like it to me." Charlie chuckled. "Lawton Pruitt's the kind of a man I admire. His own man... You really had a peculiar childhood. It explains why you are different from most of the women I meet, I guess."

"What kind of women do you meet?" She wrinkled her nose at him.

"Mostly bored, rich ladies looking for a thrill," he said candidly. "After they've done the shopping trip to Paris and the stay at the health spa, what's left? A touch of raw living appeals to them. I've had quite a few on my less strenuous tours. That's how I met my ex-wife, in fact."

"Ah-ha," said Andy with new understanding. "She played Jane to your Tarzan and it became permanent."

"For five years," corrected Charlie. "She didn't want to live in my jungle, so to speak, and she couldn't comprehend why I still did, after a while. I was supposed to want to go on to bigger and better things, although God knows what they are." He suddenly realized he was telling her too much about himself and his private life, and clamped his jaws shut, tugging at his beard. "Forget it, I don't want to sound like some guy who claims his ex-wife didn't understand him. She did. I didn't understand her; that was our major problem."

Andy liked him more at that moment than ever before. He wasn't putting the blame for a failed marriage on his former spouse. He didn't criticize her life-style, which Andy gathered was one of leisure and luxury. Charlie made it fairly clear that opposites had attracted but finally repelled each other when their differences became too great, too obvious.

She toyed with one of her braids, an idle but disturbing thought preying on her mind. Physically, Charlie was very attractive, but she wouldn't be interested in a man for looks alone. What if there was more to Mr. Wilde than met the eye? She fanned a bug away from her face, dismissing such a bizarre notion just as easily.

Three

___

Nightfall found them slightly east and far south of Tecate. Picking a spot to camp was no problem; there wasn't anyone in any direction who could object, unless the jack rabbits and toads had a say in the matter. Charlie set everyone in the party various tasks and volunteered his own talents as cook for the first night out. His generous offer was met with sighs of hunger from George and Bill, who didn't know better, and groans from Ray and Mike Morgan, who had sampled his culinary skills on previous trips.

"The one who complains the loudest has to cook tomorrow," threatened Charlie.

"Only survivors can grumble," said Ray. "How many men can boast of that?" He handed his hammer to Andy, and she pounded in the stakes to her pup tent.

There were supposed to be two people to each of the small canvas shelters, but Charlie had already made it clear he didn't expect to push equal rights to its limits with Andy.

"It's pretty," she commented, strolling over to take a cautious peek into the pot he was stirring. "The scenery, I mean. I wouldn't want to venture a guess on what your dinner menu is, from the looks."

"Watch it!" He wiggled the spoon at her, offering a preview. "You're still fresh and sassy. After a few days, you won't want to be stuck with cooking every night."

She closed her eyes and bravely took a taste. "Hot. Spicy," she gasped.

"Poison," suggested Ray Morgan cheerfully.

"Chili," hissed Charlie. "Goes great with beer. Where's George and Mike with the firewood? They should have a camp fire going or we'll have to dine and chat around the propane stove."

"It's probably better if we can't see what we're eating," muttered Andy. She had just discovered that water, bread and a sip of beer had no effect on extinguishing the fire of Charlie's chili.

The wood foragers appeared out of the gloom. Mike Morgan dropped his armload of odd sticks and twigs and presented Andy with a handful of purple lupine flowers. She was flattered by the small gesture, hoping her acceptance by the others would be as easy. Charlie raised his right eyebrow and couldn't resist a snide comment.

"Is it lupine or love in bloom?" he asked her as they began to dish out the meal. "He's only twenty-one. Be gentle with him."

"Jealous?" she countered. He snorted something inaudible and sat as far away from her as possible. She found herself stationed between Bill Wiggins and Mike.

While everyone ate—or attempted to—Charlie gave a brief rundown of the next day's plans. He described the area they were headed for, and Ray Morgan grinned, delighted at the prospect of finding Gambol's quail and other game birds. George voted for a brief stop to explore a petrified forest Charlie mentioned. Mike Morgan wanted more chili, and Bill Wiggins wanted to rub his knee against Andy's leg. She got up and moved away.

"We've got an extra shotgun and all the necessary papers and permits," Mike said to Andy. "Dad and I have plenty of fishing tackle, too. You could join us when we get to trout streams or the Sea of Cortez."

Andy fixed her gaze on Bill. "I'm not a hunter," she declared, "but I'll keep the shotgun in mind, in case I get an urge."

George Polachek was insisting they take turns telling dirty jokes. Charlie laughed and tapped his spoon for order on his tin dish.

"Ah, boys and girl, this should be a lot of fun. What is your pleasure, Andy?" Charlie asked, ignoring the old man.

"A higher altitude to watch the skies and a slightly elevated conversation," she said. "How about if everyone introduces himself and tells us a little about what he does, where he's been? Charlie, you're out of this! We know you've been everywhere, done everything and still can't cook."

"Then we'll see how good you are. Pruitt has tomorrow's dinner," intoned Charlie. A rousing cheer went up along with the hissing of pop-tops on beer cans.

Her idea of a camp fire show-and-tell was acclaimed, too. The rest of the evening was easy and full of a budding comaraderie. George Polachek was funny, although as garrulous as Wilde had noted. Ray Morgan liked to boast of every fish and animal he'd caught; he was an efficiency expert, which explained why he was impatient all the time. His son was not shy, merely overshadowed by his father and frequently told to "get to the point" during the younger Morgan's turn.

"I'm idle and I'm rich," said Bill bluntly. "To save myself from the sin of being spoiled rotten, I like to flirt with danger . . . and nature." He gave Andy a distinct wink.

"I'll save you from the sin of vanity," she offered very pleasantly. "Don't waste your winks on me." The only person not amused was Bill Wiggins.

"Pruitt devotes herself to lonely intellectual pursuits," Charlie added.

His statement wasn't completely true. Andy defended herself, explaining what she did on oil company survey trips and how she was used to working with two or three people, usually men, as they checked a region's geologic prospects for testing sites. Her field was highly technical and relatively unusual for a woman. Her listeners kept interrupting to ask her questions, with Charlie the notable exception, and they seemed to warm up to her.

"Okay, let's turn in," ordered Charlie, getting up quickly. "We rise at dawn and get an early start. We'll try to fit a full day in and make headway to La Huerta."

Andy waited until the others wandered toward their tents and watched him bank the fire. "You really don't want them to like me, do you?" she accused. "They enjoyed hearing about Wyoming and Montana. I bet I could get someone interested in the comet . . . but, no! You cut me off. What is your problem?"

He took her elbow and steered her over to the tent she'd erected. He gestured inside at her sleeping bag, kneeling to unroll his own and setting it on an air mattress. It formed the top of a T across her tent's opening.

"See?" His hand swept to the arrangement. "You'll be safe and sound from Wiggins. Or if you prefer, you can sleep in the truck and I'll take the tent."

"I don't need a watchdog. You didn't answer my question. Why were you so abrupt and rude back there?"

"Go to sleep, Pruitt," he growled.

She took off her boots and socks, stuffing the socks down into the boot toes to prevent a scorpion's taking up residence. Slowly, Andy began to squirm down into the length of the bedroll.

"You hate women!" She called from the security of her shelter.

"I love women!" He stretched out on top of his sleeping bag, fully clothed.

She realized she could never fall asleep on her stomach with her shirt buttons biting into flesh. Wriggling around, she undid them in the confined space. Her bare toes touched something alien and alive at the bottom of her bag.

"Charlie," she whispered. "Oh, Charlie."

"Don't be sweet with me," he moaned. "I don't trust you, Pruitt, when you're too nice. Good night!"

"Charlie, how many kinds of snakes are there in the Baja?"

"Besides ten species of rattlesnakes..." he began, then made a gurgling noise. "Where?"

"I can't say it is a snake," Andy answered calmly, "but I do have this guest..." She inched upward a bit, very slowly.

"Don't panic." He rolled over and got into a squat in front of her shelter. "Please, don't panic."

She was creeping forward on her elbows, holding her lower body as rigid as possible. Panic was the furthest thing from her mind. She had lost contact with whatever was intent on sleeping with her and she was not the panicky sort to begin with.

"I'm fine," she started to say when Charlie grabbed her under her armpits and jerked her straight out of the bag as if she were stuck in a drainpipe. The force of his strength sent him flying backward and landed her square on top of him, his hands clutching her in a death grip.

He scared the wits out of her. In return, Andy knocked the wind out of him.

"Son of a gun!" Andy wheezed. "Your help was not necessary, Wilde."

He made the gurgling sound again, stirring feebly under her weight. The motion made Andy conscious of her open blouse and the contact of her chest on his. In fact, there was hardly an inch of her that was not meeting some part of Charlie. She tried to get up, but his fingers hadn't loosened.

"Really, I'm fine," Andy repeated, annoyed.

"So I noticed," whispered Charlie. "That is the problem, Pruitt...the one you spoke of earlier. I love women but I rarely like one. I don't care if the others think you're the best thing since freeze-dried foods. I don't want to like you as much as I already do."

His fingers suddenly slipped under the shirt and moved on her back. His touch was light and sure, stroking down her spine to the waistband of her shorts and trailing back up to rest on the smooth skin of her shoulder blades. A slight pressure brought her even more firmly to him, and Andy felt her nipples stiffen in response.

"You said you weren't looking for love," Charlie continued huskily, lifting his head a trifle. "Well, neither am I. I won't get tied down. I can't be changed to please a woman because she pleases me."

She understood him perfectly, perhaps for the first time since they'd met. He was, like her, self-sufficient, a loner who was happy with what he was. Getting too close to other people threatened both of them and their life-styles. She didn't want to lose her independence, either, but her body was beginning to remind her of other wants, other needs.

"Let me go, Charlie," she whispered back. "You're the one holding on. You don't have to like me."

"I'm developing a passion for celestial bodies," he said. His fingers flexed but didn't relax or release her. His head rose another fraction of an inch, and she could discern his features, feel his breath. "You don't have to thank me for saving you, but I'll take a kiss."

"Like" was out. "Love" was out. They were left with "lust."

She started to squirm and lever herself off him but it was too late. Their mouths met. The wave of heat that ran through Andy was strong enough to melt the edges of her resistance. Her lips parted to object, but Charlie nibbled away the words, stopped them with his tongue. She forgot what she was going to say, momentarily.

He wrapped one arm around her and slid his other hand around her neck, holding her steady, keeping them fused along their lengths. His body stayed very still. Only the teasing and thrusting of his tongue, a slow, rhythmic invasion of her mouth, was needed to make Andy feel his excitement and her own grow.

She clenched both her hands into fists—not to hit him but because she knew she wanted to touch him and run her hands over him. He was big. Warm. Strong. He felt so good under her.

"No," she groaned into the sweet darkness of his kiss. "No, no." She was talking to herself as much as to Charlie.

He let her go instantly. Andy scooted off him and buttoned her blouse, ignoring the sound of breathing and the faster thumping of her heart. Her fingers were shaking but only slightly.

"Yeah, you're right. I'm sorry," he whispered. "I don't know what got into me, Pruitt."

"I'm going to find out what got in *with* me," Andy said. "And I'm going to throw the creature at you, Wilde."

She found her flashlight in the tent and dragged the sleeping bag outside. Charlie was right there at her elbow, but she kept shaking her head, refusing his help and his suggestions.

Andy upended the bag carefully and shook it. Nothing came out. She clamped the light between her chin and chest and shook harder. The patch of illumination jumped all over the ground until Charlie snatched the flashlight away and held it steady for her.

With a dull plop, a saucer-sized toad fell out and blinked at them both. From his grumpy expression, he didn't like the light and he didn't enjoy being disturbed. Charlie snorted through his nose and Andy began to laugh. The toad blinked again, stuck his tongue out and took a short hop toward the hospitality of the darkness.

Andy put her hand up to her mouth but she couldn't hold the laughter back. The comic ugliness of the toad and his harmlessness was part of her amusement, but she was also aware of an enormous release of tension, not fear. She had come much closer to panic in Charlie's embrace than when she was contemplating the threat of snakebite.

"Pipe down!" a gruff voice commanded from one of the other tents. "This ain't no pajama party, guys."

"You're one of the guys, all of a sudden. You're a good sport, too." Charlie jerked his head in the direction the toad had taken. "Well, I think you are. I'm going to repeat those two phrases over and over to myself until I fall asleep. There won't be any more...trouble. There won't be any repetition of tonight."

"Good," said Andy. "As long as you make the rules, you'd better stick to them. Wiggins is more talk than action, I'm sure. I wasn't worried about him."

"Do I worry you?" There was a hint of a catch in his voice.

"No, you don't," she lied glibly. Without the pressure of his hands and lips and body, she could almost believe it. "I'm after a comet, Charlie, not a man who acts like one: appearing out of the blue, staying in view for a few weeks and then vanishing."

"One of the guys. Good sport. One of the guys. Good..." He stepped away from her, murmuring as if he were convincing himself or praying to higher powers.

She pulled the sleeping bag up over her ears, exhausted and slightly frustrated. She'd got her own way—which was the rule and not the exception in her life—and she felt confused, not triumphant. All of Lawton Pruitt's drive and persistence had been passed on to her. She had used those qualities to wangle jobs that executives didn't think she could do, to compete with men in her career and her hobby, and even to be here tonight.

Her nature, like a bulldog with infinite patience, always paid off. But not in romance. From her observation and experience, men didn't want a woman who could shine brighter than themselves. They liked females to be their moon, reflecting their light and glory, or their shooting stars, flaring up brilliantly and quietly but quickly falling away when the fire was over.

Charles Wilde in a nutshell, she thought as the heaviness of sleep overtook her. *He wants a lady to be a decorative accessory for a few weeks. He wants her to exclaim over his muscles, his domain.*

She was absolutely sure of her summary of Charlie. She got her own way and she couldn't be wrong. What confused her was how much she had wanted him for one brief moment. She must be crazy.

The sun was beginning to gild the jagged peaks of distant mountains. The camp was up already with the travelers shaking the morning dew off their tents and shaking their shoes before they put them on. Ray Morgan, naturally, was packed before anyone else and, without being asked, had the breakfast and coffee scenting the fresh breeze. He beckoned the rest over to get their plates, using the fork he was scrambling powdered eggs with. Ray was a study of efficiency, never wasting a motion.

"Ray, how about riding along with me today?" Charlie asked casually after coffee. "Andy and Mike can follow. I want to hear all about that big elk you took in Canada."

"Sure," said Ray. "Why not?"

Sure, sure, thought Andy. The best method to deal with temptation is to put it far away from you. The best strategy to handle fear or self-doubt, for some people, was not to face it. After last night, Charlie would probably rather stand toe-to-toe with a grizzly bear than be thrown into her company for the whole day. She felt pretty much the same way.

"It's fine with me," she said brightly, although she had not been consulted. "Do you want to drive before or after lunch, Mike?"

Mike didn't care; he was agreeable to anything Andy wanted. Charlie wanted to know when she learned to handle four-wheel drive.

"We don't usually find oil sites along the interstate highways," Andy retorted. "So we rarely rent sports cars or convertibles, and I'm always expected to take my share of the driving."

"You could have mentioned it yesterday," Charlie said. "I drove without a break."

"You didn't ask because it's not your style. You assigned me the map and told me what to do, Boss. I was told never to volunteer."

"Sleep on a burr?" chuckled George, swigging down the final slurp of breakfast. "I heard a whole bunch of rustling around. Would have offered my help but I was afraid it was a wild boar. They come down out of the mountains, sometimes, I hear, and you shouldn't be fooled by their size. Why, pound for pound, they are the fiercest..."

"Boor," amended Andy. She wasn't sure Charlie or anyone else heard her above the drone of George's voice.

The day went well. Mike Morgan was as amiable as she suspected and, out of his father's presence, he was talkative and exuberant. He was every bit as good a shot as Ray Morgan; the number of quail Andy roasted for dinner proved it. But Mike refused to argue with his father when Ray bragged about his own skill at his son's expense at the camp fire.

Andy was tempted to speak up and say something in the younger man's defense. She wisely recalled Charlie's tactic of distancing himself from her and decided that she couldn't afford to alienate another man by her outspoken manner. Nor did she want to embarrass Mike who seemed resigned to his father's impatience and put downs. She wished he'd stand up for himself.

"Who's got the dirty dishes? I'm going to set up out in the brush and take a gander at the sky," she announced. "It should be really good in three or four days when we're climbing into Sierra Juarez and Sierra San Pedro Martir, but if anyone is interested..."

"I'd be delighted to take a peek," Wiggins said, "but I have the scullery duty. Save a spot on your dance card for me another time."

"Most unlikely," she hollered back. "The music of the spheres is a figure of speech and I can't even waltz." Andy slung her chair and binoculars off the truck and began to trudge away clutching her flashlight.

"Down, boy," she heard Charlie say. The authority and quiet menace in his tone slowed her step. She was vaguely pleased by his obvious concern for her when she remembered that his own behavior wasn't always that of a gentleman of the old school. Who was going to watch the watchdog? As she moved out of the small lighted area of fire and lanterns, she barely caught Charlie's next remark to Ray.

"How many of those little succulent birds *did* you bag? Ten or twelve? No, I guess Mike got the even dozen, didn't he? Well, didn't he?"

It was all so innocent-sounding. She grinned and walked on, amused by Ray's strangely slow and nearly inarticulate mumble in reply. Charlie didn't miss much and he didn't have to be straightforward to the point of offense, when he didn't want to be.

The night went well. No one followed for a lesson in astronomy or dancing. She had the whole marvelous dome overhead to herself, reveling in inky darkness and the clearer panorama of familiar constellations. There was no need for her to flick on the flashlight and check star charts. The bright pinpoints of light were old friends to Andy. Every star had a name and a special place in her emotions as well as in the heavens.

Her childhood had been a slapdash affair, with Lawton taking her on some of his scientific quests, leaving her behind for his forays into politics and social issues. He always returned, of course, but there were new wives and occasionally new siblings to contend with. At eight or nine, Andy felt the differences between her and other children begin to chafe.

She wished for some permanence, some stability and something to count on. She wished on a star, being a child and a young student of astronomy. And her wish came true. The beautiful objects she saw through her first telescope became her family, in a sense. Despite the many changes in her years of growing up, she could look at a night sky from anywhere in the world and be reassured that not everything was temporary and fleeting.

"Hello," she whispered to Vega, to Jupiter, to the waning moon. "Welcome," she added to the faint smudge of light low on the horizon. The comet was visible with the naked eye, and in a few days, it would be at its brightest. Shortly afterward, Halley's would approach the earth closer than any other time during this visit.

Andy got comfortable in the lounge chair and put the binoculars to her eyes. Halley's, like all comets, was a mysterious guest, not part of her regular family. She was fascinated, drawn to all comets, these elusive and largely unpredictable apparitions.

It still made her marvel to see a broad, pale tail, millions of miles long, millions of miles wide. All the scientific knowledge in her head about gas ions and dust particles did not diminish her awe. She searched for the silky streamers of light that were the tracers of magnetic field lines, but her pulse beat faster, excited by the thought of Chinese, Roman, Peruvian astronomers who had shared this view with her down through history.

You're a hopeless romantic, she mused, *masquerading as a scientist.* She had given up full-time work in a lucrative field to have uninterrupted hours to scan the sky. She preferred the company of the solar system to most humans. A lightweight object made of ice and dirt streaking faster than a spaceship made her heart race as if she were in love.

You're an impractical dreamer. If she had developed an appreciation for money as carefully as she had studied the stars, Andy could be in Australia or New Zealand or high in the Andes tonight for the best view of Halley's. But she had rushed off to Alaska to see a total solar eclipse, lasting eight minutes. She bought a new telescope. She refused a lengthy assignment for Waverly Oil so she wouldn't miss a spectacular meteor shower. Her savings evaporated until she had to settle for this trip, with all its complications.

"In my own right. I'm as kooky and unreliable as Charlie," Andy said aloud, breaking the stillness around her. She looked away from the comet and shivered. What a dumb thing to say—or even think! She glanced around guiltily and smiled with relief. She was alone and no one heard her.

Aside from their residence in the same universe, Charles Wilde and Andromeda Pruitt had nothing in common. Satisfied with her conclusion, Andy went back to admiring Halley's Comet, an unusual intruder into her stellar family.

Four

W̲ho was driving?" Charlie raised a cloud of fine dust with his shuffling around, and started to cough. He waited to let the dust settle, contemplating the ruined tire. "I must have told you people a hundred times what to look out for back there. Sharp bedrock is equal to steel spikes."

"I'm the culprit," Andy said loudly. "George was telling me a terrific story and I let my attention wander." Mentally, she wondered if she had fallen asleep for a few minutes, having been lulled by Polachek's endless recital and short on rest from watching Halley's.

"Well, get busy and fix it," barked Charlie. "We'll be camped in the foothills ahead. You can catch up when the tire's repaired. George, squeeze in with Bill and me."

"Not necessary," Bill Wiggins said. "I'll be happy to stay behind and give Andy a hand."

"I'll just bet you would." Charlie's sarcasm was thick enough to spread on bread. "You know the rules. You break it, you fix it."

"Hey, you've been kinda tough on her the past three days," observed Bill. "She strained the gasoline and buried all the tin cans and garbage."

"Shut up," Andy said. "I'm one of the guys. I can change the tire myself." She found the jack and lug wrench in back of the disabled van, expecting her willingness to end any further discussion.

Bill and Charlie were standing where she left them, staring at each other with hard, measuring looks. The others were huddled together, discussing a potential showdown in hushed tones.

"Wilde's in the right," opined George. "He treats Andy like everyone else. She can't get preferential treatment. Bill's cruising for a bruising, always making passes at her. He's not aiming to be Andy's buddy, that's for sure."

"The trout are calling my name," grumbled Ray. "They can't wait to hop on my hooks. If we don't put on more miles, I won't get my chance at 'em tomorrow morning. Hell, I didn't mess up. She did. Bill is going to get messed up, if he keeps bugging Charlie."

Andy assembled the jack and put it in place. Bill's burgeoning unpopularity had less to do with her than with his habit of worming out of any remotely unpleasant task. She resented his lazy, slack manner, too. And the constant stream of double entendre remarks he made didn't help to improve her image of him, either.

"You get in or I'll put you in," Charlie said to Bill. "I'd leave you to walk to the mountains, but Andy would end up giving you a lift, I know."

"Don't be so sure," Andy said, fitting on the wrench. She gave it a hard twirl to emphasize her statement and rocked back on her heels. "The sun's getting higher, fellows. Someone better make his move soon."

"I'd like to punch you out," Bill said loudly. He took a step toward the vehicles, though.

"You are welcome to try," Charlie invited politely. "But the effort would be too much like work, I suspect."

Andy skinned her knuckle on a tire bolt and sucked on the sore spot. She watched everyone get back into the caravan and disappear down the corrugated, bone-jolting trail. Charlie promised "rough adventure" and he wasn't lying. The Baja was rugged, desolate in many places and deserted nearly everywhere.

The peninsula had beauty in an untamed, untrammeled setting, but it took a special eye to see and appreciate it. Andy stopped to rest and looked around her, breathing deeply of unpolluted air. She liked the endless vistas, the horizon visible on every side except where the mountains loomed. She liked the weird plants with twisted and unusual forms that grew where nothing else dared. She liked Baja.

The trip was ideal for her purposes, perfect except for... *Charlie*! She loosened the last bolt and took the tire off the rim. Bill was wrong. Charlie hadn't been particularly tough on her. True, he gave her a few of the nastier, dirtier jobs like straining the day's fuel through chamois to filter out the sand and impurities, but he also gave her certain breaks. Perhaps the rest of the group didn't count how many times she cleaned up after dinner, but Andy had. None. Charlie knew she was eager to get to her chair and her sky.

When she took him aside the other night and asked if he was doing it deliberately, she got a lopsided grin and an immovable man. "Cooking. Washing dishes. Those are the traditional women's jobs, huh?'' Charlie asked softly. ''I didn't want to be accused of stereotyping you.''

''And what if the others accuse you of playing favorites?''

''Pruitt, flatten all the cans and go bury the trash again, will you? Bury it deep so no animals can dig it up.'' Charlie strolled off, whistling.

No, Charlie wasn't being mean or singling her out. But there was an unspoken tension between them and it grew stronger every day. She could feel it coil tight as a watch spring in her abdomen whenever Charlie glanced at her and then looked away quickly, silently. He kidded and quarreled with her when the rest of the men were present but he also managed not to be alone with her even for a second. When he handed her a map or a spoon, he made sure there was the most minimal contact of his fingers and hers, short of throwing things at her. He stepped out of her way if she was anywhere near him, and yet Andy got the fleeting sensation inside that they had touched.

In another week, she speculated, we'll be circling each other warily like wolves or snapping at each other's heels. Strain would become irritability and inevitably argument.

She tightened the final nut and bolt of the spare, rubbing her hands together in glee and slapping the van's side in self-congratulation. It was impossible to get separated from the main party. The ancient, dry riverbed road she followed was deeply trenched into the rising hills until it ended in a pile of gigantic boulders, like a child's heap of tumbled blocks. The others were camped at the foot of Sierra Juarez, part of the peninsula's mountainous backbone.

She climbed out of the van, dirty and bedraggled and damp from her solitary struggle. ''Have any trouble?'' George squinted at her. ''You look like something the cat drags home.''

"Thanks." Andy grimaced. "No problem. Where's Charlie and Ray?"

"Scouting us the best streams to fish. Up there in the pines." George made a vague gesture above his head. "As soon as Mike's done, you might want to go wash in the spring, or whatever the puddle we found yonder is."

"The grimier, the better," Andy said blithely, thinking of Charlie's avoidance of her. If she smelled and looked like a mountain man, no one would wonder why he didn't want to ride with her. She envisioned herself tied to a fender like a prize deer and smiled. At least she could catch up on her sleep.

Her resolution weakened as soon as Mike came into sight. He was as pink as a cherub, freshly scrubbed and beaming from ear to ear. "It's great," he confirmed, waving a greeting to her. "It takes a shortage of fresh water to make a bath seem like a big deal. And the stream's not freezing, either. I was sort of hoping it would be deep enough to swim but heck, you can't have everything."

"Some of us can't have anything," Bill complained laconically from the shade of a tree. He didn't bother to direct the remark to Andy or explain it, and she really wasn't listening to him.

She rummaged through her disordered suitcase and found a complete set of clean clothes, a towel and soap. Mike jerked his thumb back over his shoulder, starting to give directions to the spa, but Andy was past him, scrambling over the rock-strewn path.

She let out a small squeal of joy when she spotted clean, running water. It was scarcely two feet wide, well hidden in a thick tangle of spiny bushes and weedy head-high grasses, but only a hot shower would have looked better. She shed her grubbies in record time and didn't bother to check the accuracy of Mike's report with her toe before she flopped in.

The water was not freezing. It was ten degrees above freezing. It was not deep enough to swim in, but it was hardly deep enough to get completely wet in, either. She was face down in three inches of very cold mountain water.

"W—ww—wonderful!" Andy chattered cheerfully, sitting up. She lathered the soap and smeared it on, trying not to notice how blue she was turning. Goose bumps as big as the Rockies, or pneumonia, were not going to worry her. It was never a week between baths on oil survey trips and there were usually motels around with a few amenities. She wouldn't count on a better chance in Baja.

Clenching her teeth, she went for broke, washing her hair with bar soap and rinsing it in ice water. There were noises in the rocks off to her right, but by the time she cleared the suds off her head and out of her eyes, it was quiet. Very quiet, in fact. The birds she had heard before had flown or fallen silent.

An animal, she guessed. Any stream would attract local wildlife. She wasn't going to sit and die of exposure to observe a mountain goat or sheep or puma up close. A furious buffing with her towel restored circulation and made her as rosy as Mike. She put on her panties and was diving into her T-shirt when the noises started again.

She heard panting and growling, the sighing of grass and snap of underbrush. Finally a howl of pain emerged. She easily recognized a series of human yelps. Involuntarily, Andy froze and listened until there was no further crashing and thrashing.

"Hey, everything's okay. Go ahead and get dressed." 't was Charlie's voice, but there wasn't anyone in sight. He sounded out of breath and almost cheerful. "See you in camp."

"You've already seen me!" Andy shouted back fuming. "You miserable sneak, I hope you broke a toe." She pulled on her jeans, bundled her dirty laundry and didn't bother to lace her boots, she was in such a rush, driven by outrage.

She would kill him. No, she would humiliate him and tell the others what a creep Charlie Wilde was. He'd been playing Nature Boy too long if he had to get his thrills peeking through bushes.

She could hear a hubbub in camp before she saw anyone. She put on a burst of speed and charged, ready to finish Charlie off. She found him coolly sipping at a beer, propped on a rock, and taking in the sights of Sierra Juarez. Bill Wiggins, lying prone on the ground, was moaning intermittently between lots of loud, excited comments from the others standing over him.

"Charlie!" Andy bellowed in what she hoped was a peal of thunder. He turned his head and met her eyes directly. Seeing his face, handsome and composed and utterly guileless, prevented her from compounding a mistake. She lowered her voice. "What happened back there?"

"An unfortunate accident," he said with mellow baritone regret. He sighed, reached down and popped the top of a second beer, holding it out for Andy. "Today must be a low cycle, biorhythmically speaking. First, you and the tire. Next, poor Bill and the thorns. They may hurt now but wait until they have to be yanked out."

She took a few steps closer to Charlie and extended her hand tentatively. "He fell into stickers? Near the stream?"

"That's his story," Charlie said evenly. "He may have chipped a tooth, too, although I don't see how a stumble in the weeds can do that."

"What a pity!"

Their fingers became linked but she didn't take the beer, and Charlie didn't withdraw his hand. There wasn't any cockiness or gloating in his voice; he sounded genuinely sorry, a tinge of disgust coloring his voice. There wasn't any mischief in the dark brown eyes locked with her blue ones, but Andy couldn't name what she saw.

"Don't be mad...at anyone," he said. "Getting punctured a few dozen times let most of the wind out of Bill's sails, I think. We have a long road yet to travel. It'll be better if we're on speaking terms—all of us."

"Okay, I won't hold a grudge," promised Andy. Her own indignation had mysteriously drained away. She realized she believed Charlie and, even more amazing, admired him for handling the situation the way he had.

A major confrontation in front of the others would have forced Bill into showing how tough and fearless he was or backing down again, losing face. Either course of action would make for bad feelings and a bad trip. A minor, private skirmish allowed Charlie to make his point in a telling, painful but not dangerous manner and avoid any escalation of hostility.

"We're almost even, aren't we?" Charlie gave her hand a small squeeze and then let her stand there, holding a beer at arm's length and staring at him.

"I don't know what you're talking about," Andy denied but she suspected she did. "Maybe I should go over and offer to help Bill. Just to show him there aren't any hard feelings."

"Suit yourself." Charlie jumped down off the rock as Andy started to back away, and stood toe-to-toe with her for a long tense minute. "If I underestimated you, Andy, you haven't done much better in your assessment of me, have you? In her unkinder moments, Jane used to accuse me of being nothing but an overgrown Boy Scout. You didn't even give me as much credit as she did when you came roaring up the wash a few minutes ago. I'm a lot of things, not entirely cheerful, thrifty, reverent and good, but I'm definitely not a sneak or a voyeur."

She could feel heat and color creeping into her neck and face. She hoped her tan would hide such a childish, unbecoming flush but she didn't try to cover up her embarrassment or the truth. "I am sorry, Charlie," she said sincerely. "I did think the worst. I apologize."

"Accepted." He fell into step with her as she attempted to make a tactful retreat across the encampment. "You and me, Pruitt . . . we ought to start over on a different foot. It's not so bad scrapping with you but it might be nice to be friends. How about it?"

"I'll think about it," Andy said, giving him a suspicious sidelong glance. "I admitted I misjudged you. That does not make us blood brothers, however. Don't try to kid me. You still have some serious doubts about my abilities to fend for myself."

"Luckily for you, I do," Charlie rumbled. "You would have had a great time keeping Wiggins in control with a towel and a bar of soap."

They reached the men clustered around Bill. The guilty party looked up pitiably as Ray Morgan tugged out one sharp spine after another with a pair of pliers. Andy's "all is forgiven" speech had to wait until the yowling died down, and she fully intended to set Charlie straight.

"I don't require a bodyguard," she said hotly. "Never have. Never will. All right, you happened along at the right time and in the right place. You saved me from a big scene and some aggravation but . . ."

"He was just worried about you." Ray lifted his head and gave Bill a chance to calm down. "I told Charlie you could probably manage the tire and you hadn't gotten lost. There wasn't any need for him to cut our stream hunting short to drive back and rescue you." He went back to his doctoring. "I told him."

"What?" screamed Andy. "He was going to do *what*?"

Charlie was waving both hands feebly "Best intentions... safety first, y'know...."

"Don't get mad at anyone! If I underestimated you, Andy..." She quoted Charlie's own words back to him with a vengeance.

Ray, Mike and George lost all interest in Bill's predicament and watched, openly and raptly, as a new drama threatened to unfold. Bill Wiggins breathed through his mouth and managed to look silly and sheepish, simultaneously.

"Friends," continued Andy, feeling more comfortable with anger at Charlie than gratitude. "Friends generally think each other capable of carrying water in a pail. I can't be friends with a man who thinks I'm a jerk, afraid of dirt and a toad, simply because I'm a woman. You wouldn't have dreamed of driving back to check on Ray or Mike or George or Bill."

The list of names ran her out of breath and she couldn't continue without a respite. Charlie grabbed her upper arms and thrust his face inches from hers.

"Okay, okay," he whispered hoarsely. "Give me a break, Andy. You aren't a jerk. You aren't Jane. Let's kiss and make up. Do anything you like but please, don't throw me in the briar patch!"

The men guffawed and visibly relaxed. Andy's eyes widened and her mouth dropped open a fraction of an inch. She wanted to finish this argument, once and for all, but she chuckled instead. He was the craziest, most exasperating man, whether he was being solemn or silly, capable or cuckoo.

"You're impossible, but we do have a long road to go together. Let's call a truce," she said, but she puckered her lips up in an exaggerated fish face and squeezed her eyes into two thin slits. No one wanted to kiss a carp, she assumed.

"I'm improbable," countered Charlie. "You're impossible." Before she could duck her head or twist away, he kissed her with a loud, resounding smack.

Andy hadn't been expecting him to call her bluff; she was only teasing him back. She became acutely aware of the men's laughter and comments. Someone was assuring Bill his reputation as Don Juan was safe if Charlie couldn't do any better than that. *He can,* she thought with a peculiar sinking feeling, remembering their last kiss.

Charlie must have been recalling a past encounter, too. Her quick perusal of his face showed a dreamier, darker quality in his glance, a slight arch to one of his eyebrows. Charlie said nothing in his own defense as Andy walked away.

She was almost grateful for the light misting of rain that began at dinner. The day had exhausted her physically, and the events of the afternoon had left Andy as emotionally drained. She was happy to avoid everyone's company and retire to her tent early; her book, a flashlight and a candy bar had more appeal tonight than George's camp fire anecdotes or making polite chitchat with Bill. The skies would be better tomorrow, she told herself philosophically, and curled up with her dog-eared paperback.

Charlie, their fearless leader, returned from the stream and made his usual ruckus setting out his bedroll. Andy turned a page and shut out the sounds of his nightly routine. Once the drizzle started, Charlie had announced that he might as well take a bath.

"Pruitt?" came his quiet query. She didn't bother to answer. "Andy?" he persisted. And finally, "Andromeda?"

Marking her page with a finger, Andy listened to the faint patter of rain on the canvas and answered. "What is it?"

"I want to talk," Charlie said. "Can I stick my head in there and let my hair dry?"

"I know, I know," she murmured. "You just washed it and can't do a thing with it. Charlie, I don't feel much like talking."

She flicked the flashlight off a fraction of a second too slowly. Charlie's shaggy head popped through the tent's flap, and the sight of him registered in her brain as the darkness closed around her. Andy snapped the button back on and gaped at him. Without a beard, Charlie Wilde was not raggedly attractive; he was downright handsome.

The lower half of his face was, naturally, pale and rather strange-looking, contrasting to the even tan above. But his features, particularly his wide mouth and strong jawline with a suggestion of dimples at the corners of his mouth and the flare of sturdy cheekbones, had never been so impressive hidden under his thicket of beard and mustache.

"What in heaven's name prompted this?" she asked. "My gosh, Charlie, you look . . . well, you look fine."

He smiled, evidently pleased with her verdict. "Speaking of looking fine, there's a brook up higher, not far from Laguna Hanson, that I'd like you to visit tomorrow. It's got all the earmarks of a great trout stream in a little forest clearing. Terrific view, too. You can see the universe, I swear."

"Really?" She brightened immediately. "If the climb isn't too steep, I'll take my stuff and camp up there."

Charlie gave a short nod of assent. "I figured you would. You've got to see this place, Andy. Shallow mountain lake, tall Jeffrey pines, and massive granite boulders tossed here and there. How about fishing in the morning?"

"You and me, fishing . . ." She paused to see if she had heard him right. They had a truce, not a peace treaty, she recalled. "The whole kit and kaboodle of us, right?"

"Naw, I staked this one out for myself. Let the others find their own. Of course, if Ray insists on joining us, I'll have to let him.... He was with me when I noticed the spot, but it would be great for us."

For us? *Us?* Now she was really confused, but pleasantly so. Charlie was taking the offer to kiss and make up seriously and including her in the group, not avoiding her. Fishing buddies wasn't a bad notion, she decided. She had some experience with Lawton when she was younger.

She gave her head a small toss and then shook the hair out of her eyes. "It's been a long time since I did any casting but sure, I'll give it a whirl. That's nice of you, Charlie. Real nice."

"You make it sound like a miracle, my being nice," he said blandly. "Have I been all that bad?"

She wasn't going to let him off the hook too easily. The only sound for a while was the dull sporadic plop of raindrops on her tent. "You've been watching me pretty closely," she said slowly, "and hoping I'd foul up to prove you right. You're a tad irritated, I think, that the trip's going as well as it is, Bill Wiggins aside."

Without asking, Charlie scooted more of himself into her domain. It got very cramped and cozy, and there wasn't any escape for Andy. She held her ground and her breath, wondering what this was all about. Charlie was nothing if not unpredictable.

"I've been thinking..." Charlie began softly.

No one ever looked so good, so sweet, so sincere, she thought with a twinge of desperation. Of all the men in the world, she was faced with Wilde, who was determined to live up to his name, and she liked what she saw. Worse yet, Andy glimpsed within herself the awesome rippling light of another emotion. She was falling in love with Charlie Wilde, a man who was as colorful and insubstantial and fleeting as the northern lights.

"Lord help us," Andy murmured. She focused her gaze on the patch of night visible behind him, stunned by this revelation.

"I *do* think from time to time," Charlie said, misunderstanding her plea. "If I'm not as deep as the men you're used to, I'm not entirely the macho jock you've pictured."

He was hurt. Inadvertently she had touched two sore spots in Charlie today and saw that he could, indeed, be hurt. He was a man of action and instinct, but any intimation that he was lacking in intellect stung him. By choice, he lived an outdoor life, one of natural struggles and survival, but it rankled when he was labeled as primitively or childishly simple.

Andy raised her hand slowly and rested her fingers lightly on his cheek, the skin smooth and cool. It would be easier—and more sensible—to go on pitting wit and will against Charlie. She was opening herself to unexplored territory if she cared for him.

"You aren't stupid or simpleminded," Andy whispered. "I respect you, Charlie, for what it's worth."

His hand covered hers, engulfed it to hold it to his face. "It's worth a lot," he replied. "I like you, Andromeda Pruitt, and I like your style. That's why I was thinking it's silly to ignore you or pretend you're a drag on the operation."

"Thank you, Charlie," she said, matching his seriousness with her own. "I'm beginning to appreciate you, too."

"Friends?" he asked, echoing his earlier question. There wasn't any note of levity now. There wasn't any glint of humor in the rich brown of his eyes.

"Friends," she repeated without hesitation.

She let him pull her hand down and hold it. Charlie studied it, from her skinned knuckle to the chipped fingernails, turned it over and held on. Andy waited for his handshake, the closing of this agreement in gentlemen's fashion.

He muttered two words. She didn't catch them clearly, but it sounded vaguely like "thank you." Something "you," anyway. Whatever his final words, he puzzled her even more when he pressed his lips to her upturned palm in a very brief, tender kiss. Then Charlie backed out, disappearing more rapidly than he had appeared.

With her flashlight off, Andy held up her hand but she wasn't able to see it or even to make out its outline. Her palm felt warm, and when she pictured Charlie's head bent over her, the heat traveled into her heart, a small, secret fire deep within her. The tenderness and simplicity of his gesture had moved her.

The rain had stopped and she listened carefully. She couldn't hear Charlie stirring or snoring but she knew he was out there, close in the night. Close enough to hold.

But not for long, warned her mind, banking the fire and longing to know him, understand him. There might be many hidden facets to Charlie. As his friend, Andy could do more than merely glimpse them. She closed her hand tightly, folding her fingers over the spot he'd kissed.

Behind her closed eyelids, she saw his clean-shaven face, split with a grin at her compliment. He hadn't explained why he'd done it, but she knew with the certainty of intuition. He had shaved to be admired, to please her.

He cares what I think. What I feel. Oh, my. What else does he want? she mused fleetingly, and before she could ponder the question, she fell asleep.

Five

After seeing both low and high desert, Laguna Hanson appeared closer to paradise. It was a genuine mountain lake, more than five thousand feet high in the plateau country. There was a respectable amount of shining water in it due to a heavy runoff of winter snows, but Charlie said that after a while, the lake would be little more than a wet meadow until the late summer rains came. Wilde's tour was not the only visiting, admiring group at the highly accessible lake.

There were more people dotting the edge of Laguna Hanson than they had seen since Tijuana. Early bird pic-nickers and campers had already staked out the few rustic tables and fireplaces provided by the government. There were actual trash cans, rare and notable objects in Baja, marking the only public recreation area of its kind on the entire eight-hundred-mile peninsula.

Andy was carrying more gear than anyone else. She was determined to find her ideal nightwatch post to camp up here in the piny forests. Welcoming the chance to talk to someone besides the Wilde bunch, she hiked around part of the lake's marshy shore, stopping to introduce herself to several groups.

"No other *norteamericanos*," she announced as she re-joined her companions. "There's a German couple on an extended honeymoon, an enormous Mexican family from Ensenada and a shrimp boat owner from San Felipe. He must be on a busman's holiday because he showed me tackle large and sturdy enough to snag Moby Dick."

"What are you?" inquired George grumpily. "Our am-bassador of good will? The census bureau? We're here to catch fish, not take a head count. Forget all these peo-ple..."

Polachek's voice trailed off as he stomped away, pre-pared for a solitary quest for fish. Mike and Bill had al-ready vanished.

"What's eating George?" Andy asked Charlie and Ray. "It's not like him to be so snappish."

"Too many foreigners," postulated Ray. "George needs new listeners for his stories and you brought him the bad tidings. No one else here speaks English. Although, to tell the truth, the language barrier shouldn't stop him; they'll probably be a captive, polite audience and every bit as at-tentive and interested as we are when he really gets going."

Andy shook her finger, scolding fashion, at Ray, but she chuckled. George was a world-class bore if he had an ear—any ear. They let Charlie lead the way, a few paces ahead, while she and Ray tried to figure out a diplomatic strategy to deal with George's loquacity.

His tendency to ramble on and on was increasing as the days and miles flew by. What had been funny a week ago was wearing thin by now; nobody wanted to be stuck driv-ing for hours on end with George and, short of a gag or earplugs, no solution seemed feasible. Andy was envied because she had a good excuse for slipping off almost every night while the rest of the party endured the telling and retelling of George's stories.

"Maybe he doesn't realize how much he talks," she interjected charitably. "Someone could tactfully suggest that there's nothing wrong with peace and quiet."

"Maybe his wife and family are deaf," Ray said, cackling to himself. "I wish I was."

"Knock it off!" Charlie ordered, glancing back over his shoulder. "All your jabbering won't muzzle George and you'll scare away the trout. Leave him alone."

She and Ray traded puzzled looks. Several evenings, they had seen Charlie chewing the inside of his cheek to bite back his own frustration and annoyance with George Polachek. Charlie made no secret of the fact that he had no use for people who talked to hear the sound of their own voices, or the "civilized" habit of having music, radios and TV's constantly humming in the background.

Ray obeyed, dropping his canvas duffel and climbing on a rock ledge to survey the twisting shallow stream ahead. Andy was too curious about this apparent change of heart to let the subject drop. She followed Charlie upstream until they were out of Ray's earshot and she persisted in a much more subdued tone.

"I don't understand," she admitted. "You dealt with Bill's negative influence rather handily. I suppose George's yammering isn't the same thing. Granted, the old gentleman does his share without a peep of complaint and he isn't likely to assault me or you or anyone. But, Charlie, what'll we be like after three more weeks of his unending verbal history of Polachek?"

"I doubt George will make it all the way to La Paz," Charlie answered. "He's lonely. He's homesick. As soon as he figures it out for himself, he'll fly back to San Diego. He talks to fill up his own emptiness, Andy."

Until yesterday, Andy would have been maddened, infuriated by Charlie's surety and quick analysis. Today she was less convinced that Charlie's perceptions were snap or spur of the moment judgments. He didn't act hastily or speak as casually as it had first appeared to her.

"Are we going to fish or fuss?" he asked suddenly with a suggestion of a smile for her. "Bet I get one before you do."

"Oh, yeah?" She struck a mock-defiant pose, hands on hips, and stuck her tongue out at him. "What'll you bet, master angler?"

"Anything," Charlie responded instantly. "Anything you want."

His statement sounded innocuous, but the stark hunger on his face contradicted him. The offer she saw shining in the darkness of his eyes was anything but innocent. Andy felt as if he were reading her mind with ease, reflecting back what was printed there in secret. They shared their mutual secret in silence, knowing how much they wanted each other, unable to say it.

She was frankly shaken by the desire she saw briefly. There was nothing aggressive, nothing she should reject. Charlie's look was one of yearning—a full and sweeping need—and it was more than physical in origin. For a split second, he was allowing Andy to see him naked, emotionally, and she saw both a terrible loneliness and a nameless fear.

She wanted to touch him but was afraid he would misinterpret any contact. She wanted to tell him she understood, and was sure he would deny it or make the moment into a joke. She didn't know what to do except treasure his offer of himself and his trust in her.

"How about if I take your oil-and-water maintenance duty or you take my chef's assignment, depending on who wins?" Charlie's suggestion of stakes came out haltingly. He actually stammered a few times in his effort to bridge the awkwardness.

"All right," agreed Andy, eager to concentrate on something ordinary and safe. She made a feeble attempt to be light. "That way, if you win, everybody wins at dinner."

"No one can ruin fresh trout," Charlie said, and the spell was broken. He was already testing his reel, giving his wrist an experimental flick to see how limber his casting arm was.

Andy chose a spot downstream from him and not too close to Ray's rocky outpost. She stood staring into the sluggish current for a long time, watching the water for telltale ripples. When a trout broke the surface and snapped at a hovering insect, she decided she would look less like a fool if she was, at least, going through the motions of fishing. She didn't particularly care if Charlie won their bet; her usual high spirits at the prospect of competition weren't there.

She fumbled through the borrowed collection of wet and dry flies, and tied on a scarlet and gray one without paying attention to which type it was. The flow of the water picked up speed over a series of small drops, and she aimed her cast there. The thin line flew out, fell and was carried to a rockier place. There were small nooks and niches for fish to hide in. Over and over, Andy cast and watched her line drift until she drew it back without success.

"Well, I'll concede the stream looked good." Ray's voice broke her meditations. He came toward her, complaining about this waste of his time. He wouldn't stand around when there weren't immediate results. "I want trout, not postcard scenery. I'll just ankle over and see how Mike and the rest are doing. I gave Mike my best flies, anyway. Charlie hit a clinker, picking this place, and I'm going to tell him so.''

Charlie had chosen well, Andy thought. Fishing had other rewards than the catch. The sport was as much for contemplative time as for thrill and action. Ray was missing a lot more than just trout; he might have discovered vital facts about himself if he would hang around longer, look into the currents running through him.

Fish weren't impressed with how rich or poor the fisherman was, how clever, confident or efficient he was. It took patience and skill with a healthy dose of luck. Nothing guaranteed you the prize, and unless you could walk away empty-handed and still say, ''It was great,'' and mean it, there wasn't any joy in fishing.

Her thoughts seemed to spread out in ripples from her original idea. Whatever her relationship with Charlie became, it wasn't simply a test of wills or a battle of the sexes any longer. They were sharing with each other: companionable quiet, the depths of this stream and part of themselves. When the trip was over and they went their separate ways, she would be able to say, ''It was great,'' and mean it.

''Glory be!'' She hollered at the heavy pull on the line and the arching of the rod's flexible tip. ''Gotcha!''

The water swirled into a white froth with the trout's thrashing. Andy felt her heart speed at his first wild run from the strike and then fade almost as quickly. After the hook was set, she only had to haul in the gleaming, dappled trout. She held it up high, showing it to Charlie, but she was also confirming her own thoughts. Catching the wily creature wasn't as fruitful as fishing for it.

''Good for you,'' came Charlie's congratulations. He threw her a salute from his clump of bushes and flat, stacked rocks and went right on casting. ''What'll he go? A pound and a half?''

"A pound, tops," Andy called out. "Not dinner for six, that's for sure. Let's get lucky and get some more."

Hours later, Charlie called a halt to the morning's activity. He had two fish in his creel, and Andy had snagged two more. It wasn't remarkable bounty, but they retraced their steps to the lake in high spirits. Charlie lied blatantly about a mythic four-pound monster that nibbled several times at his hook. He claimed the fish rejected it only because Andy always coughed or sneezed or moved at the most inopportune moment.

"Tell me another one," encouraged Andy, giving him a playful punch in the shoulder. "I love a creative liar. You sure you weren't born in Texas? Now, this trout was a female, you said. I didn't know you could tell such things, scout."

He gave her a solemn nod and threw his arm around her shoulders, pulling her close. Their legs moved smoothly, brushing together, giving her a warm, pleasant feeling.

"Of course, it was a lady trout. She couldn't make up her mind. Fooling around, fiddling around. Looks good, she says, but not that good. She heard you snorting downstream and thought you were making fun of her, so she took off."

"Aw," groaned Andy in mock sympathy, "you must be so disappointed! The biggest and best ones always get away through no fault of ours."

Charlie stopped in his tracks and both his arms circled her, shedding creel and rod carelessly. He tilted back his head and gave her another smile that took her breath away as quickly as his phantom fish fled. "I'm not disappointed, really. I'm in complete agreement with Henry David Thoreau. 'Many men go fishing all their lives without realizing that fish was not what they were really after.'"

And what are you after? The question rose naturally in her mind and Andy was ready to ask it, seeing clearly that Charlie would answer. Those little circular ripples of her thinking seemed to have intercepted similar waves from Charlie.

"Charlie," she said. Only his name emerged, but she put all her longing, her loneliness and her heart into the sounds. There was far too much to ask him, but saying his name and seeing him, as if for the first time, was a start. *I love you. It's too soon, it makes no sense but there it is.*

"Yes," Charlie replied in a very quiet but definite voice, although she had said nothing but his name.

It struck Andy that she was asking a question and he was answering it. She swayed closer, moving against his hard body and into the closing ring of his arms. His head descended toward hers, their lips slightly parted in anticipation. Sooner or later, they would be lovers.

"There you are! Whoops, I didn't mean..." George, of all people, never came on any scene silently. He muttered to himself if no one else would listen. "Excuse me all to hell..."

Andy and Charlie both jumped guiltily, startled back to reality. George was backing up, bumping into trees, righting himself, and talking a mile a minute.

"Getting late, yes, it's late, and we...that is, Ray and Bill have a fire and coffee started. I was coming to get you. See what was keeping you," George babbled. "But if you don't want lunch... Mike caught a two-pounder."

"It's okay, George," Charlie broke in reassuringly. He released Andy and scooped up the fishing tackle. "You saw what was keeping us and it'll keep a while longer."

Charlie stirred up the red-gold embers with a long stick to make the fire blaze. The intricate play of light and shadow on Andy's face was worth watching awhile longer. He kept finding more to marvel at in her and it was his nature to appreciate beauty wherever and whenever it occurred. She'd bound her hair into a moonlight pale braid that swept across her shoulder blades as she turned, answering Mike's question, giving another of her impromptu lectures on the comet.

"April eleventh, Halley's will be a mere thirty-nine million miles away from the earth." The bright blue sparkle of her eyes flashed. Her hands fluttered gracefully to show the position of the comet, its orbit. "For this return, that's its closest approach. My photos won't be able to touch the ones taken south of the equator, but I've been setting up my camera on the telescope anyway."

She explained how more of the comet could be seen on a long-exposure photograph than through her telescope or binoculars, due to film's ability to store up light. George felt compelled to interrupt with a rambling tale of his family's vacation where thirty rolls of film were later developed to reveal he had left the lens cap on.

"When we get to San Felipe, you can get your pictures processed and not have to live in suspense," suggested Charlie. When she acknowledged him with a smile, a peculiar soaring sensation filled him. He fought it down, suppressing the lightness with effort, knowing what it was.

Love. Charlie peered into the flames, determined to control his own fiery thoughts and needs. Love? The last thing he was looking for in his travels had come to find him. His first words, spoken in jest, when he saw Andromeda haunted him. "I think I love you."

"I'm off to my ridge," announced Andy, standing up. "Anyone interested in using the binoculars while I'm adjusting the camera?"

Bill declined, quickly. George was too intent on recounting the building of a hydroelectric dam he'd once designed to look up at her, much less the sky. Ray accepted, leaving Mike as George's hapless victim.

"What about you, Charlie?" She paused at the very edge of the flickering circle of light and looked directly at him. "Don't tell me one or two sightings through my telescope satisfied your curiosity."

The muscles in his calves bunched, ready to stand and accept. But the tightening in his loins told him too clearly that he wasn't as eager to see the cosmos as be with her. This afternoon his promise—that what was keeping them locked in an embrace would keep a while longer—had to be honored. He'd made the promise as much to himself as to her. Perhaps Andy did not entirely understand what he'd meant, but Charlie did. It meant "go slow" and "watch out."

"Thanks, but I'm busy planning our route for next week," Charlie said huskily. "It's too bad we can't all steer by the stars. Go ahead! Have a good time and don't catch a cold out there."

The high, thin air was much cooler. He could offer himself to keep her warm. He desperately wanted to, and Andy might well accept tonight. In fact Charlie watched her leave, aching to follow, knowing that they were already lovers, waiting only for the right moment to confirm it. Such knowledge disturbed him as much as the vision of her gilded by the firelight or the sound of her saying his name aroused him.

His premonition of Andromeda as beautiful trouble was coming true. She was no shallow, silly creature anxious to amuse herself with him, as a few others had been. She was not Jane, titillated by his differences and distance from her wealthy, social world, playing the goddess until she grew bored. Andy was special, a phenomenon as rare and attractive to Charlie as Halley's Comet was to her.

Back in San Diego, Charlie must have known, instinctively, that Andromeda Pruitt was very nearly his perfect woman. He avoided facing it only by avoiding her as much as possible. But she'd got to him in a very short time. Her capable, confident manner, her strength and her humor pierced through his pretense of disinterest.

They had started off badly, shifted to polite indifference, and now were behaving like good friends. It was the pattern of his ill-fated marriage in reverse. Soon they would want to bow to the inevitable, giving expression to their desire for more, much more. Charlie was afraid, a state he barely recognized.

What if loving her was too good, too great to let go when he moved on?

He was avoiding her tonight but for very different reasons. When he finally held her in his arms and showed her with his body how he felt, the delicate balance of understanding they'd established would crumble. He would reveal to Andy with every stroke of his hands, every thrust of his hips, every low endearment, the solitary lack in his life: a perfect woman to share it with. His perfect woman.

But he could never give up his life-style, not for Andy or anyone, not even if he had to be alone and lonely the rest of his life. The very qualities he admired in her—independence, self-sufficiency—were the ones that would make her reject him and his love. He was afraid and avoiding a dilemma of his own making.

It was easier to plot a route through Baja than to untangle his own twisting, tangled emotions. Charlie's yellow marker skimmed down the map he was studying.

"Boy, you ought to mosey out there and take a peek," said Ray. He propped his elbows on the fender Charlie was using as a desk, and lit a cigarette. "Andy must be some terrific teacher. She can calculate directions in degrees using her mental yardstick and tell you the magnitude and name of any star you point to. Bright, organized woman! If she went into a decent business, she'd be rich."

"Maybe she's not after big bucks. Money isn't everything to everyone," Charlie said out of the corner of his mouth. Part of him no longer believed it. His ex-wife said he had the business sense of a chipmunk and she was right.

"It beats whatever is in second place," Ray said. "You know, Charlie, if you expanded these little tours of yours, your volume would offset the expenses better. Twenty people would make you a nice profit, allow you to buy more equipment and have to lease less. That's efficiency."

"It's also impersonal, generally. I don't want to herd mobs through the Yukon or the Grand Canyon. I don't want to drive a bus through Baja loaded with passengers and tell them when to look right, look left. I get to know my people and the places I travel with them."

Ray Morgan assumed the clipped, brisk speech of his professional role. "I can show you how to double your business. I've watched your operation firsthand three times now and I'd invest in Wilde 'N Free myself if you'd listen to me," he boasted.

Charlie folded his maps slowly, precisely, and stuck them in his back pocket. "I don't have partners because I don't want them, Ray. I have to answer only to myself and my clients. And the only way I'd double my business is to develop a split personality. But thanks."

He closed the conversation by walking briskly to Andy's empty tent. The exchange with Ray hadn't taken his mind off Andy but reinforced his train of thought. People couldn't leave well enough alone. They had to change nature to suit themselves, carving roads everywhere, to make their travel convenient. They changed hair color on a whim and ethics for a dollar. Change didn't mean progress to Charlie.

He rubbed the stubble on his cheek and felt foolish, hypocritical. He'd shaved to make Andy look at him twice, see him as someone other than a hairy ape. Well, he drew the line at other changes that were direr threats to his freedom—like love, like marriage. He had the whole earth to explore, and it was slow-going for any man chained to mortgage payments, insurance premiums and bills for the orthodontist. George Polachek was a man like that, saving up for his one big fling with Charlie, but unable to relax and enjoy a horizon too wide after too long a confinement.

The night was very long. Andy did not come back. Charlie told himself a thousand times he was not going out after her. If she wanted to sleep in a webbed beach lounge and let the dew condense on her, fine. She could have had a deck chair on the North Star with a steward tucking a plaid blanket around her, a cup of steaming bouillon on a silver tray. She was entitled to her eccentricities, and Charlie wasn't interfering with or changing her. Live and let live, thought Charlie irritably.

The sky reddened slightly, a false dawn before the sun actually rose. He rechecked the luminous dial on his watch in disbelief, listened to the experimental trill of a single bird who immediately quieted. Where was the damned woman? Eaten by a bear? Frozen into a lovely ice sculpture? He couldn't fall asleep. Not because of her, he hastily decided. There were tree roots under his air mattress. There was a scent he couldn't identify on the morning breeze. As the leader, he was responsible, wasn't he?

He went, bearing gifts, out to the wrinkled ridge she had stationed herself at. His boots made no noise on the thick carpet of pine needles, but with each step, the earthy, vanilla fragrance rose up around him. Andy was asleep in the folding lounge, her big binoculars in her lap. Charlie set the cup of coffee down next to the chair, kneeling close himself to study perfection in repose, a real Sleeping Beauty.

Throw the blanket on her and go. He gave himself an order, started to obey, and ended up touching his lips to her forehead. She stirred but didn't wake. Her mouth moved soundlessly, a tiny pulse throbbed at the base of her throat, and the rise and fall of her chest was slow, peaceful.

Draping her in the folds of thin, scratchy wool was easy. Taking his hands away from the curve of her side, the slight rise of her hip and the incredible length of her legs was very difficult. Leaving her was out of the question.

Charlie wasn't sure how long he sat there before the pale fans of her lashes fluttered and she saw him. There was a bleary confusion when Andy's eyes swept around the forest and she realized she wasn't in her tent. Understanding replaced bewilderment, though, when her hand ran lightly over the blanket. Her lips twitched, curving up in a smile.

"Hey, sleepyhead," Charlie asked gently, "how did it go last night?"

Stiff and groggy, she tried to sit up in the chair and sent the binoculars skidding off her lap. Charlie's hand grabbed and caught them before they hit the ground.

"I overdid it," she confessed. "Halley's didn't grow two tails or split up into a million billion shiny fragments, but I couldn't take my eyes off it. This—" her nails scratched at the blanket "—was sweet of you, Charlie."

"I brought you a cup of coffee you could tar a roof with, too." He lifted the tin mug and grimaced. "It's ice cold, sorry. You should have taken that cruise ship deal when you could."

"And miss breakfast in bed?" She laughed sleepily but stopped herself, giving Charlie a look that drove the morning chill out his bones. "And never meet you? I think I got a far better deal with you, Charlie."

He had reasoned with himself during the night, warned himself to put on the brakes before anyone got hurt. He reminded himself that a man with the self-control and discipline to live anywhere in any conditions could handle the urge to love one woman.

Charlie knelt by her chair, leaning into her and easing Andy back. He traced the pale arch of her eyebrows with one tentative finger, moved down her sunburned nose to rub the soft inviting line of her mouth. The contact was slight, tenuous, and yet he felt the electricity of it run through him.

"I want you," he said simply. "I wanted you before I knew your name, Andy. But I also like you. I care about you. And when this trip is over, I don't want you to have any regrets or bitter memories of me. I was awake all night, wrestling with what's right and what's wrong."

She was listening, eyes wide, and taking in every word. Her lips opened very slightly and her teeth nibbled at the end of his finger. Charlie forgot what he was going to say next. He frowned instead.

"A comet's getting very close to the earth," Andy said in her sexy, throaty voice. "It's too rare an opportunity to miss." She ran her tongue lightly over his finger.

"Halley's?" A surge of current flashed down his spine, gathering power in the small of his back. He rocked forward to steady himself and found, instead, that he was touching her, stroking and caressing her. His brakes were definitely slipping.

"You," breathed Andy. "I want you, Charlie. I spent most of last night dreaming with my eyes open, watching one comet but wanting another."

He knew he was fallible and weak, and she set him off course, careening without caution or any need to talk. He would give her anything in the world she wanted, take her any place she wanted to go. She rose, arching into the pressure of his hands on her breasts, and her arms drew him down to her.

His deep, lingering kiss was welcomed, returned. Her taste was sweet and clean, like spring water, and no matter how long he drank, his thirst for her was stronger. There was no need for him to hurry because she clung willingly, pliant under him, her mouth taking as well as giving Charlie pleasure.

When he shifted his weight to take away the blanket, Andy's small whimper of disappointment made him tremble until he understood. She was actually afraid that he was leaving. *No, no,* he wanted to tell her, *we've been rushing toward each other on a collision course for two weeks now.* What they were doing was as predictable and unstoppable as her precious, magnificent comet.

Her sound became a softer hum as he opened her blouse, spreading it wide to allow his fingers and then his lips to roam slowly but ceaselessly over her breasts. Where the sun and wind hadn't touched her skin, she was as white and smooth as polished ivory. He trailed too many damp kisses to count over every inch of her exposed flesh until he thought he would devour her in his hunger.

"Charlie," Andy whispered urgently. Her fingers kneaded the muscles of his shoulders, climbed up the back of his neck and buried themselves in his hair. "Oh, Charlie, wait!"

Wait? His tongue flicked over a pebble-hard nipple, feeling her tremble. He couldn't wait to discover much more, to taste the special, secret flavors of this woman. He thought his body would burst with wanting, his head would split. There was nothing but her, the faintly sweet and totally natural fragrance of her body's own perfume, the heat rising into him from her skin.

Wait? He would die or go mad.

"Wait?" Charlie gasped hoarsely, lifting his head to see her face. She was serious. He stood up, unsteadily and in an obviously aroused state. "Andromeda, we are miles from the nearest cold shower."

"Oh, Charlie," she said in a small, thick voice, choked with regret, "we're miles from a drugstore, too. I'm sorry but I certainly didn't plan for what almost happened to happen . . . and I don't want . . . well, I do want but . . ."

If he wasn't half-crazy, the fog would have lifted sooner in his brain. He squirmed uncomfortably and gaped at her for a long painful moment.

"Ah-h-h," he exhaled, finally putting one and one together and realizing the sum in her head was three. "I'm the idiot, Andy. Oh, darling, I'm going to make love to you but I don't intend on taking the chance of giving you a souvenir of Charles Wilde you don't want. Believe me! There's as many ways for a man and a woman to make love as there are stars in the sky, aren't there?"

"There are?"

Her surprise was so genuine, it couldn't be faked. Charlie stared for a second at the most nearly perfect half-naked woman he had ever seen, and she stared back. He ached too much to explain. He was too surprised and mystified himself to ask any questions.

"Andy," he said softly, "take your clothes off and come over here." He spread the blanket out on the pine needles. He began to unbutton his shirt, undo the fly on his jeans and kick off his boots all at once. "We still have a lot to learn about each other."

Six

She didn't move, and Charlie made no attempt to go to her. Clothed only in the thin, pale ribbons of morning sun, they simply stood there in the quiet clearing and looked unabashedly at each other. She could have easily believed she was still dreaming; all the elements of an enchanted encounter were here: a man so beautifully formed, naked and powerful, with a longing as equally unclad in his eyes.

But it was real. Charlie was a reality hard to dispute, solid and tall and sculpted for the touch of her hand. Her fingers opened and closed, unbidden, at her side, eager to hold him tightly. Excitement, sharper and hotter than she could ever remember, flared in her stomach and along the insides of her thighs until she shifted her legs in anticipation.

He saw. He understood. The quick, audible intake of his breath and the perceptible throb of his aroused flesh signaled to Andy in eloquent, primitive ways.

"Let me love you," he said hoarsely. "Please. Now!"

She would not have refused if it meant the earth would stop spinning. Stretching out on the blanket, she raised both arms, her mute plea to touch heaven and embrace a man like a comet.

He lowered himself onto her, his weight and length a good anchor to hold on to while the sensations rose.

She was guilty of lying, inadvertently. Her claim that she was not inexperienced with men was being rapidly disproved. Every lingering kiss from Charlie's hungry mouth, the bolder and bolder exploration of his hands, was a totally new experience. Little gasps of pleasure rose and escaped from her throat.

He searched out her hidden places, an unhurried teasing that made Andy call his name and clutch at his shoulders. The hard contours of his body pressed into her thigh and when she moved her hips, unable to resist joining the regular rhythmic pattern of his caresses, he groaned and moved, too.

His lips closed on the aching tip of her breast, nursing hungrily. Andy arched, losing herself in the quicker, more insistent demand of his fingers and mouth. A cry of wild abandon shattered the quiet, and the demand of her body, fully alive, took over.

"Oh, yes," she whimpered, "yes, yes." Her stomach clenched as if in fear that the awesome feeling would never end. Each feathery brush of his lips took her closer and closer to an almost unbearable tension. "Please, Charlie."

"I will please you," he whispered hoarsely before the promise of his mouth was demonstrated. The heat of his breath melted her, the sweep and dart of his tongue drove her to frenzy.

She gave herself over entirely to the tremors that shook her, hurtling her into the farthest reaches of her soul. Like a star, she felt herself blaze in fire, shine with incredible brilliance and nearly explode with the power he'd released.

She floated weightlessly in his embrace, unaware of how long a time she lay there. It seemed forever and yet it must have been only a few minutes. Charlie kissed her again and again, his hands gentle on her, and his body reminding her of his own unfulfilled needs.

"I want to please you, too," she murmured almost shyly. "I was selfish . . . not thinking."

"You are wonderful," Charlie said thickly. "And beautiful. And the most exciting woman in the universe. You don't have to do anything. . . ."

"I want to," Andy whispered, matching the words to deeds. She smiled at him and saw the dark fires flicker in his gaze. "I want to touch you."

Just as boldly and sweetly as he had touched her, Andy found what could delight him. "This?" she asked, thrilled not to be passive, reveling in his responses. "This?"

She pursued whatever was good for Charlie, learning him more intimately than she had ever known a man. She thought he was beautiful, too, the epitome of a totally unashamed male, unselfish as the aggressive lover, trusting and content under her hands.

With a violent shudder and a soft moan, he found release and held her tightly to himself. His face nestled in the sheltering curve of her throat, and they soothed each other's damp, exhausted flesh with light touches, barely felt kisses.

The morning breeze dried them, and the birds' faint chorus returned, gaining strength as the sun gained height.

Charlie's face left the sheltered valley of her breasts, and an anxious expression replaced one of blissful contentment.

"Oh m' God, everyone's been up for an hour. They'll know we weren't out here counting craters on the moon. Hurry up, get dressed, honey."

It had been weeks since he called her that particular endearment. It didn't make her bristle this time, but his unseemly haste in leaping out of her hug did.

"Keep your pants on!" she said before the full humor of her remark hit. She giggled and reached for her clothes. "Well, too late for that. Charlie, where's the fire?"

"We put it out," he said with a sly grin. "Look, we're going to have to behave ourselves. This development has to be handled right."

She did a double take and halted her fumbling with buttons and zippers. "That's a funny thing to say and a weird way of putting it. Development? Behave ourselves? To begin with, I don't think we did anything to be ashamed of. Second, I wasn't planning on dancing back into camp with a sign saying, 'I slept with Charlie.' Ah, 'slept' is imprecise and inaccurate. The word is..."

"Don't," Charlie ordered angrily. "Don't spoil it with pretending our lovemaking meant nothing. That's not what I meant and you know it. I was thinking about how this can change more than just our relationship. I'm aware of how men react on these all-male jaunts and, if you care to recall, I warned you about a woman being a potential sore spot. I didn't know I was going to add to the problem."

She smirked at him, finding a new source of energy in her annoyance. "Sore spot! Problem! You sure can sweet talk me, Charles. We were lovers ten minutes ago."

"We still are," he said, grabbing her for a fast, final bear hug. He checked her fly and straightened her collar before heading her into the trees. "I'll come back and get your stuff later. Let's go...and let me handle any comments when we get there, okay?"

"I wouldn't let you handle watering my plants," grumbled Andy. "These strange, inexplicable attitudes of yours make me wonder why I care about you so darned much. Could you please explain exactly what is bugging you?"

"Not me—them," came his cryptic reply. "Some men get touchy and irritable when they're deprived of female company."

"Horny," Andy summed up.

"Yes, you might put it that way. I didn't want to put more stress and strain on this group; nature gives us plenty to handle. I'm no advocate of secrecy. I'm concerned with discretion and the smoothest operation of this trip."

"Oh, for pity's sake, Charlie! George isn't interested, Bill's been subdued and Ray and Mike aren't about to misbehave with each other around. There's no need to worry."

The more they argued, the longer their strides got. Charlie crashed through the underbrush, busy detailing the dire consequences of male jealousies and competitions.

"You notice, I didn't go hunting when they did. I went fishing with you, but just once. I've seen it happen, Andy. They pay me and want me to be leader when it comes to guiding them but they don't want me to be a better hunter, a better man. Wiggins is going to think you would have naturally gravitated to him—rich, good-looking, smooth— but I interfered."

"You did, thank goodness." She stumbled on the rock-strewn path and caught herself in time, refusing Charlie's hand thrust out to help her.

"Ah-ha, you see, you were glad I intervened. You wouldn't admit it before. That incident was another illustration of what I mean: you look to the leader to handle the problems, not to create them. You resent some of my decisions, but I'm right."

She threw her hands up in disgust, breaking into a trot to keep level with him. "Have it your way. You are the infallible trail boss, the master of woodcraft and psychology. I'll act as if nothing happened."

Charlie clutched her around the waist and jerked her to a halt. "We didn't plan it but it happened. I'm glad."

"I'm not so sure I am," Andy said. "I really don't care what anyone thinks or knows about me. But we could be discreet and sin no more. No sneaking a hug and a kiss!"

She tugged free of his grip and darted down the steeper bank of the ridge, steps ahead of him. Charlie's ability to nettle her rivaled his skill at loving her. She heard him panting after her, cursing colorfully, and understood that this was a mutual ability. They set off all sorts of fireworks without much effort or striking a match.

"Well, I wouldn't swear it won't be repeated," howled Charlie. "I'm crazy about you, Andromeda Pruitt."

"Be discreet," she flung back over her shoulder. "Shout it louder!"

He actually did try, defiantly, at full volume. "I'm craz . . . zz—"

Missing his footing, Charlie's head dropped suddenly from her line of sight. He plummeted down the slope, skidding and landing on his butt, sliding along with a huge quantity of loose dirt and stones, and landed in a shower of dust at the base of the ridge, about ten yards ahead of her.

He was feeling himself gingerly when she rushed over, calling his name, caught between hysterical laughter and tears. "Are you all right? Charlie, talk to me. Tell me."

"I'm crazy about you," he repeated dazedly.

"No, no," cried Andy, brushing ineffectually at him and peering into the pupils of his eyes to see if he was suffering from concussion. "How do you feel? Did you break anything?"

"I fell halfway down Mount McKinley and didn't break anything," growled Charlie. He regained his dignity by pushing her hands away and getting to his feet under his own power. He took a trial step with the hint of a limp but kept walking. "I broke my wrist in a cave in New Mexico once. Two ribs in British Columbia in a kayak."

"You *are* crazy," she agreed, keeping pace with him. "You're so concerned with looking after everyone else, you seem to have forgotten to take care of yourself."

He held up three fingers for her, shaking them under her nose. "Three serious accidents in as many years. That's not so bad. Not one of my clients got more than a bump and a scare."

"It's not so great, either," countered Andy. "I saw the scars on you, Charlie when we were . . . well, before."

"Scrapes, bruises, nothing much," he said airily. "I'm doing fine."

But when she put her arm around him, he didn't seem to mind and even listed into Andy a bit, letting her take some of the weight off his right leg. They arrived at camp and were greeted by Bill.

"Cozy picture," he said snobbishly. "Did you two win the three-legged race or the potato sack event?"

Charlie shot her a look of pure triumph, a real "I told you so" glance, and took a step sideways. "Fell down a hill," he said shortly. "Took a while to get back."

Bill was dubious but silent. Andy curled her lip in disgust and left. Male pride and gamesmanship were beyond her fields of interest.

Charlie was living dangerously, in more ways than one, if he thought she would ever play by his rules. To keep peace? To preserve his image?

Andy heard him barking orders for the loading of the caravan; he was testier than ever. His ankle was probably killing him, she thought ruefully, but he'd do twice as much just to prove there was nothing wrong.

Having seen him as a tender, vulnerable person made her like him more. His sudden concern for appearance made her distrustful. She wouldn't hide it, tuck it away as if love was a weakness. She'd broken a few rules of her own on this trip, and she wasn't feeling regretful, merely aggravated. Charlie was worth loving but he took a fierce effort to understand.

"Deer. Wildcat," said Ray to her, walking by and rubbing his hands in glee. "You don't know what you're missing, Andy, by not taking up hunting. The challenge!"

"My life's directed toward 'search,' not 'destroy,'" retorted Andy. Her jaw was firm and determined as she steeled herself, preparing to join George as his passenger. "I've been on the hunt, in a manner of speaking, for as long as you have."

"Planets, comets and shooting stars," dismissed Ray. "You can't catch one of them and tack it up on your fireplace mantel to show what you stalked long and hard and outwitted. No trophies."

There were no trophies in astronomy, she knew, but were there winners in love? It was unlikely George or Ray or any man would understand her if she asked. She'd have to find the answer to that one for herself.

A Charlie Wilde, like Halley's, didn't appear on her horizon every day. It didn't bother her that he would neither be caught nor held by any woman; she would judge for herself how fine, right and regular Mr. Wilde was and where his orbit was taking him. She felt better again, her usual confidence restored.

"What are we waiting for?" Andy asked when George refused to start the engine.

Polachek screwed up his face and took off his baseball cap to scratch his thinning hair. "Are you suffering from exposure or what? Wilde went to get *your* gear, not mine. I thought he was being awfully solicitous of you, but that guy's pretty sharp. There is something wrong with you."

"And something right with him," Andy said too softly for George to hear. She drummed her fingers on the dashboard in a nervous little tattoo. She couldn't believe she would forget her precious equipment for all the gold in Crete.

Charlie had forewarned them about the next leg of the journey to San Pedro Martir, but until they were under way, no one had much faith in his description. The sandy stretches trapped two of the vehicles, and the following rocky ascent slowed them to five miles an hour. There had to be frequent stops to change drivers before their ability to concentrate completely failed, and to allow everyone breathers from all the jolting and sliding around.

"Best looking country I've seen," allowed Bill Wiggins at one break, "and I spent a couple of months in the Alps last year. If they bothered to run passable roads in here, they'd draw the tourists."

"It's supposed to be the clearest spot on the continent," said Andy hopefully. "Can we drive much farther, Charlie?"

She was searching the jagged peaks ahead for a sign of the new national astronomical observatory located on one of them. It was not open to the public, except on a very limited basis, but she was confident she could talk herself into an admission.

"There's logging roads on the western slope," he said. "The eastern side is so steep, we'd have to be able to fly. This route will take us up near the ranches."

He got a laugh for what they took as a joke. Deeper in the rugged foothills of the mountain, it turned out, there were two large ranches: a working cattle ranch of a pioneering family, and a guest resort, each with a small private airstrip. The rest of the range was designated a wilderness area, and no hunting was permitted. Charlie had made arrangements for his group to hunt on the privately controlled lands.

"The logging roads can't be as bad as what we've covered," Mike said to Andy, who was frowning at El Diablo's pinnacle. "You'll get up there somehow, knowing you."

"Burro or backpack," Charlie put in. "The logging roads are badly deteriorated and poor, to put it mildly. Buck up, though! The better the place in Baja, the worse the roads. The southern half of the peninsula will seem like traveling a four-lane highway once we get past Santa Rosalia."

"He means, *if* we get there," grumped George, slapping dust out of his cap onto his thigh. "Pruitt, you drive the next hitch. Heights make my nose bleed, and from the look of that winding grade ahead, we're not leveling off."

"Fine," declared Andy, climbing back in, "but if it's too steep and scary, I'm going to close my eyes."

She ended up wishing she could. The sharply precipitous drive made roller coasters seem tame, and the driver had no choice but to keep both eyes wide open, dodging fallen rocks and washed-out holes. The route he chose was the shortest, Charlie said, but she would have liked one that was a trifle flatter, less winding and narrow.

"I'm...old," George stuttered out between the plunging and rising of the Jeep. "Death's...not such...a tragedy...at my age. You might want to reconsider...grab a plane..."

She geared down and fought the steering, sending the Jeep into another hairpin curve and bouncing the wheels back from the sheer drop. "I'm not...a quitter, George. If I have to...I'll hitchhike with one...of these eagles that...keeps flying by us."

"Those eagles are vultures," he cheerfully informed her.

"But...but this is the apex of the trip for me!"

In a minute, Andy thought disconsolately, *I will begin to whine and pout and stamp my foot.* She opened her hand and gestured at the men clustered around Charlie. They ignored her nonverbal appeal and went right on with their impromptu council.

"I didn't see so much as a rabbit," confirmed Mike. "Dad and I covered three...four square miles and talked with everybody we bumped into. The road construction crews have flushed out the game and sent them to parts unknown."

"Hardly seems fair, considering how tough it was to get here." George rubbed the seat of his pants to illustrate his point. "It's pretty here but it isn't worth having my tailbone twisted and my teeth shook loose if all we can do is sit around and twiddle our thumbs. I'm with Ray. Let's get going."

Andy charged the group, ready to do battle. She had missed a perfectly clear sky last night due to a late arrival, the general exhaustion and the necessity of her pitching in to help set up the camp. From the sound of things, she wasn't going to get another chance...ever.

"Now wait a second," she said hotly. "It's not even lunchtime and you're already paying the check, ready to skedaddle out. We're supposed to spend a couple of days..."

"Hot pursuit of a cold woman is a total waste of a man's time, effort and hormones," Bill drawled. "Stalking anything that won't cooperate rarely pays off any better."

She gave him the dirtiest look she could muster up. "You guys can't have covered the whole mountain in one morning."

"Tell her what the man on the Sierra Club outing told you," urged Ray, elbowing Mike. "Go on!"

"Uh, we met these people on horses, packing through the high country," Mike began reluctantly. "They've been up here nearly two weeks and they haven't seen any game, either."

She focused her annoyance and upset on Charlie. He was listening and not bothering to say a word, his arms folded across his chest, his head tipped slightly to one side. He knew how important this scheduled stop was to her, even if the others didn't. Why couldn't he speak up and support her? Was that too indiscreet?

"Charlie, you look like a cigar store Indian," she ground out between clenched teeth. "Tell them. Speak! *I* want to stay, according to the Wilde itinerary. What do you say?"

"It sure is nice that they're finally building roads," Charlie said dutifully. "One to that observatory you think is such a nifty addition, Andy, and one for guests of the ranches. Me, I always oppose nice roads through wildernesses because they scare off the game and spoil the very nature of the land you're trying to preserve." He glanced at Andy. "There! I told them."

She pushed George out of her way and marched stiff-legged over to where Charlie was standing. She jabbed his midsection with her finger. "I was not asking for your opinion of the modernization of the Baja. I wanted your decision as our worthy leader that we stick to your schedule and stay."

"I know what you want," Charlie said evenly. He inclined forward and whispered to her. "And I know what I want. But it may not be possible." He straightened up, appraising the mood and faces of the men gathered around them.

She fought down the shivery, tickly feeling caused by the warm caress of his breath in her ear. The notion of leaving was horrible. The nonchalant way Charlie was acting was equally awful. But the realization that she was helplessly, hopelessly affected by him was the worst.

As skillfully as he had avoided her earlier, he had found a hundred legitimate reasons to stand near her, touch her casually, help her move this or that since they left Sierra Juarez. He managed to hover around, a continually potent reminder of what had transpired, while behaving irreproachably.

At this rate, Andy decided, she was going to lose her mind as well as her choicest viewing of the comet. They were sometime friends, one-time lovers, and there was no indication that their status was heeded by the others. Charlie, however, kept up his charade that she was "one of the guys" and nothing more. It was beginning to tell on both of them.

"Majority rules," claimed Ray. "I'm not being mean, Andy. But the rest of us have rights."

"And nothing in our sights," chimed in Bill. "There's four others to consider. We're for going where the action is."

She started to present her case for staying longer. Hadn't she put up with their detours here, there and everywhere the first week in the desert? She hadn't objected when they stopped at the petrified forest for George or the hot mud spring for Mike's photos. The higher the altitude, the better for her and all she wanted was two nights more.

"I say let's pack up and get a move on right now. We could be in San Felipe that much sooner." Ray looked around the circle expectantly. There was a second from Bill, a noncommittal shrug from George, and Mike avoided her eyes, not wanting to alienate her or his father.

"I'm still the head honcho," Charlie said softly. "I didn't put anything to a vote."

Bill stopped arguing with Andy to swivel his head toward Charlie. "Four against one, Wilde...or two? Don't side with her just because she's got the prettiest legs. What will we do for two more days and nights?"

Charlie ignored the snide comment, pinching the bridge of his nose, deep in thought for a minute. "Well, okay. Here's my solution. We'll stay tonight so Andy gets her chance. The rest of us can go over to the Sky Ranch, relax and play some cards, hear some music. Tomorrow, we'll leave."

"They got a bar? Ice cubes?" asked George.

"They've got a steak dinner and a refrigerator," Charlie said with a conspiratorial wink at Andy. "They've got a radio patch setup with the States, too. You could call home, George, if you wanted. If we get there early, we can rent some horses and take a ride."

He'd hooked George and Mike both with hardly any effort. They were nodding agreeably. Ray was adamant, and Bill looked distinctly bored and disinterested.

"Well, you two could take off ahead of us," said Charlie. "Nothing stopping you, if you're set on going."

"Those logging roads are hell, you told me," Ray objected. "They branch off every which way. There's only one pass through Martir. We don't know this country. We'd get lost for sure."

"Yeah, probably," agreed Charlie. "That's why we have to stick together. Otherwise I would have left Andy with a Jeep, wouldn't I? Say, Bill, how about a little high stakes poker tonight? You're a big roller. Penny, nickel or dime?"

And it was settled. Andy didn't have the nerve to carp about being cut to one night. She had been sure their vehemence would outweigh her desire. Charlie had handled it beautifully, she admitted to herself. He used the right amount of authority and compromise, bribery and appeal to fair play. He didn't rise, externally, to the bait Bill cast at him to make the decision a personal issue.

"Thanks, Charlie." She mouthed the words across to him and got another wink.

She wasted no time. At dusk, as soon as the men were preparing to drive to Sky Ranch, she hiked off. It was close to five miles for a great view, but there was no possibility of taking one of the vehicles. Most of the distance was up over several stony knolls and grades.

The sky was so good that she hated the thought of leaving. Two hours went by before she checked her watch and dragged out the star atlas to make sure she didn't miss anything of interest. A drop of water splatted on the paper and she brushed at it. Another drop fell. She took notice of the weather for the first time, the approaching banks of clouds, a drop in temperature.

The wind gusted, bending the trees in violent jerky motions. It howled through the branches and sent up miniature tornadoes of dust and dirt, swirling around and pelting Andy.

"Rats," she said, craning her neck to peer at the near sky, abandoning the long view. Her ankle stung where a stone grazed her. The clouds would ruin her evening's plans.

It was not supposed to rain during spring in the Baja. Not more than a mild sprinkle, anyway. A flurry of fat raindrops hit her upturned face in direct contradiction to the guidebook description of the normal weather.

She hastily covered the telescope, packed the binoculars in their case. It would blow over in minutes, she thought firmly. She sat crosslegged on the lounge and prepared to wait out the storm.

The clouds had not read the guidebook, it soon appeared. She was drenched in five minutes, wringing wet in ten. There was no letup, the rain coming down in flat sheets. The thunder didn't budge her, but the spectacular streaks of white and pink lightning decided the matter. She didn't want to be struck out in the open or flattened by the nearest falling tree.

She was doubly agitated, picking up her equipment and preparing to retreat. The night was the only one in San Pedro Martir she'd get and it had been a concession to boot. She'd thanked Charlie too quickly. His finagling had been wasted, and her gratitude premature. The night was a total bust!

"Your cooperation would have been appreciated," she flung at the heavens. The rumble of thunder reminded her of Charlie's grumbling tones. A startling and brilliant flash of forked lightning made the night into day for a terrifying instant.

The path she followed up was rapidly becoming a streambed, slippery and difficult to walk. Andy slid, fell, and got up, keeping the telescope dry at all costs. She jumped clear of floating pine branches and landed calf-deep in a soggy, muddy spot. It was no problem to wash off. Within a few more minutes of trudging, the downpour of rain had showered her clean.

She reached flat ground and, chest heaving with relief, propped the chair on a tree. The camp was, presumably, steps away. She pushed her sopping hair back off her forehead and peered through the rain and ground fog. The camp did not appear to be where it was supposed to be. She looked back at the trail she had just covered; it was a slick, fluid squiggle on the mountain.

"Lost," she said aloud, testing the sound of the word. The boom and crash of thunder ate up the squeak of her voice. "I believe I am lost."

In principle, she was in fine shape. The camp was near, she assumed. It was either north or south of the place she was standing. She was not thrilled with the prospect of picking the wrong direction and tramping through water, wind and ankle-deep bogs for the rest of the night, however.

She draped her blanket, doubled, over the chair and scooted down under it's minimal protection to consider her options. She was sure of only one thing; she could not get any wetter, clammier, colder or more peeved. She watched three hours of unrelenting rain tick off on her watch. Tendrils of fear, too, were taking root and growing in her. She didn't like being alone and lost and miserable.

"Anybody home?" asked Charlie, cheerfully, before the thunder drowned him out.

Seven

Andy lifted a corner of the sodden blanket and peeked out. His boots, caked with mud, confronted her. She let her eyes wander up and, when the lightning flashed the next time, she confirmed that it was, indeed, Charlie, a monstrous black silhouette against the momentarily bright sky. Unmistakably Charlie!

She squeezed and squished her way back out with a helping hand from him. "Nice of you to drop by," she said pleasantly. "I wasn't expecting company. What happened? Did the poker game end early?"

"Wiggins cleaned me out in half an hour," Charlie said, "and it started to rain. I got scared, thinking about you up there by yourself."

Her little facade of nonchalance crumbled. She grabbed Charlie and buried her wet face into his equally wet shirt-front. "Oh, ick," she summed up. "Get me out of here and to someplace dry, please, Charlie!"

His lips came down on top of her head. "I would love to, Andromeda, honey. There is a small hitch, however."

She looked up, trying to see in the gloom. "What is that?"

"Ah, well, you see, the rain has washed out my tracks. The storm has flash flooded most of this area and—"

"You're *lost*, too," she interjected. "Charlie, you are telling me you came out looking for me and now you're lost!"

"Not *lost*," Charlie objected loudly. "I am temporarily disoriented, shall we say. It can happen to anyone in extraordinary circumstances."

The rain stopped for a minute, then resumed as if the sky were hiccuping. Andy doubled over with laughter, enjoying his discomfiture as much as humanly possible.

"Oh, I see," she howled. "I love it, Charlie. I'm the stray, you found me. Now where are we?"

"Lost," he said with a huge grin. "No need to panic, Pruitt. The worst thing to do is rush around in the dark and bust an ankle."

"This is the most fun I've had in years," she swore. "Whatever this trip is, it isn't dull. Thanks, scout. What do we do next? I'm pretty sure both of us can't fit under the chair and, anyway, it's not a very secure port in this storm."

"There're some rocks over there," he said, sweeping his arm in a vague arc. "Not a cave, actually, but a hidey-hole we could wedge into until this stops or lets up. Once I get my bearings, we'll be on the right path in no time."

"Or over the nearest cliff," Andy mumbled to herself. However she was far too damp, and her teeth chattered too loudly to encourage argument. She let Charlie steer her toward his refuge.

As a shelter, it was just slightly a cut above the chair. The space she wiggled into was taller than it was wide or deep;

it could have accommodated her alone nicely but it wasn't designed for two. She and Charlie jockied for a comfortable position, discovered there was none, and ended up sitting, face to face, legs wound through and around each other, knees high enough to rest their chins on.

"Hey, it's dry," Charlie said before she could make a snotty remark. "Relatively speaking, of course." He shifted slightly to fumble for something in his pocket. The minor move jammed his leg more firmly between her thighs and pushed her back harder into the unyielding rocks.

The pressure of his leg felt rather nice; the texture of the stones did not. "Ease up, scout," she complained. "We can't dance in here, that's for sure."

There was a flare from a struck match. Charlie held the match and his waterproof kit aloft, and smiled beguilingly at her.

"May I offer you a complimentary piece of chocolate, a needle and thread or my antivenom equipment?"

"I'd like a different table, closer to the window," she said. She wondered aloud how long they would be staying.

The match blew out as he pressed a square of foil-wrapped candy into her hand. As soon as the storm was over or the light was up, whichever came first, Charlie promised he would have no difficulty retracing his steps to camp. He insisted the best thing to do was to relax, pass the time in chitchat and to remove her sneaker from alongside his rib cage.

In the dark, he sighed with relief when she complied. It became very quiet with only the sound of rain, the crackle of the foil and their breathing, still ragged and labored from the rush through the storm.

"It was nice of you to arrange tonight for me." Andy was becoming uncomfortable in the dark, listening to him, sensing his presence and body so strongly. She couldn't stop thinking about a morning not long ago, a lovely clear morning in another mountain setting. "It's a shame it didn't work out, but that's not your fault."

"I'd like to travel with you . . . alone . . . someday," Charlie said. "You could do all the things you like. I would like to show myself sights and not have to always mediate between what this one wants to do and that one wants to see."

His hand came to rest on her knee, rounding the curve of it over and over. She put her hand over his, linking their fingers in a tangle as tight as their legs.

"That would be fun," she said. She thought for a minute and added, "Or it would be a disaster. Charlie, why do we fight so easily?"

"We're a lot alike, maybe too much." His answer came back so quickly she knew he'd given it consideration before. "We're both stubborn, used to doing it our own way, and protective of our territory—ourselves. I'll bet you got hurt badly when you were little, if not lately."

There wasn't anything to do or any place to go. Andy let her head find a less bumpy spot behind her and rested back. She started talking about Lawton and her childhood, how lonely it was, how muddled and transient it seemed.

Charlie listened without interrupting her. After a while, she almost forgot he was there. There was only an occasional movement, the faint scent and warmth of another human to remind her. She told more than she would have normally, letting him know how hard she found it to commit herself completely to people, always afraid they, too, were temporary. Friends, lovers, siblings—everyone seemed to change and move away.

"Is that why you get so angry with me?" Charlie asked when she was finished. "Because you know we're together by accident, for a certain amount of time?"

"I guess," she said reluctantly. "It's over before it's begun. We shouldn't care too much about each other with the end in sight. That, and your insistence that we playact indifference in front of the others. I'm no good at acting, Charlie. I say what I think and I show what I feel."

"You're right," he said. "Acting brave and cool when you're not is a big deal for men. It doesn't work for me where it concerns you. I didn't play poker tonight, Andy. It started to pour as soon as we got to the Sky Ranch, and I told them I was going out to find you, that I was afraid you'd get hurt or hit by lightning."

"So they know..." She stopped, struck by the fact that he'd hunted for her for five hours in a torrential downpour.

"They know I care for you," he finished, "and they know I don't care if you blister my ears about treating you like a woman and someone special...because you are. And I wish you were my woman. Just mine, only mine."

She sat absolutely still, not quite believing she'd heard him right. He wasn't joking, acting brave or cool. He was telling her some painful truths; she could hear the strain in his voice, feel the tension in his legs.

"I thought you had a different lady on every tour," she said. "I thought that's what you were offering me. You, as part of the package deal."

"I am. If and when you want me, for as long as you want me," he said. "I can't offer more, Andy, because I don't have more. I haven't had affairs with many women; I just don't bother to correct that impression or deny any rumors. It's sort of protective coloration."

"You were so flip about your marriage," she said softly. "I thought you were a woman-hater or a Don Juan."

There was bitterness, undisguised, in his voice this time. "I'm a babe in the woods when it comes to females. I was raised to be the polite, chivalrous gent. I was always awk-

ward with women, not sure how to take care of and defer to
them. If you want to really laugh, you should see me at a
cocktail party with sophisticated ladies.''

She tried to see past him, to check if the night was over.
Being Charlie's confidante was not without its own dis-
comfort. She became aware of how much she cared for and
wanted him. She was swept up once more by passion and
longing but there was no way she could pretend it was a
mistake, something that ''just happened.''

''The weather's not so bad now,'' she rasped, hinting at
a quick departure. A commitment was too easy for her to
make, sharing secrets and lives this freely.

''It's worse than it's ever been,'' Charlie replied. ''I'm
conscious of being thirty-four, a bum to some and playboy
to others. I can be *me* with you, Andy.''

''Oh, Charlie,'' she said, burying her face in her hands.
''Please stop before we both say things we're sorry for.'' It
was half a plea for him to stop and half for him to continue. She understood they were doomed as lovers. The
knowledge hung before her like a curtain, thin enough to see
him through, thin enough to touch him briefly but too
strong to ever be torn down.

''I don't have any regrets,'' he persisted. ''I hope you
don't, either. I want 'us' to go on together, openly and as
long as possible. I want you to say yes or no to me.''

Too late, her heart thudded to her. *Too late to turn back.*
Charlie brought everything out into the open in the most
cramped, godawful place she'd been in. He wasn't her life-
long companion of dreams; he was Charlie. He wasn't offering eternity but the present.

Andy could calculate distance in trillions of miles, time in
millions of years, but Charlie Wilde fit into no equation
she'd seen. They could not postpone goodbye, but she was
unable to say no and postpone any more love in her life.

"Yes," she whispered and had to say it louder for him. "Yes, I'm not sorry about what happened."

"I wish I could kiss you," Charlie said, "but I'm scared to move. I think it's going to take a shoehorn to get me out of here."

She turned, her body inched closer to his, until she was facing the same way and almost next to him. His arms fastened around her, drawing her back into the planes and hollows of his body. Charlie's lips brushed the back of her neck, fully expressive of the tenderness he felt and found it hard to speak of. His hand moved lazily along her length, melting away the need to consider their future.

There was now. They were happy and good together. She closed her mind to anything else, tipping her mouth up for a kiss, willing to open her heart fully to him.

The morning arrived before the rain stopped completely. The drizzle didn't hamper visibility, though, and Charlie wanted to prove his tracking skills. Before they left the rock shelter, he slapped the granite with a friendly pat.

"Great spot," he said. "I must mark it on my map."

Andy crawled out and groaned. "I won't forget it soon. My spine has turned into a pretzel. Quit smiling, Charlie, and help me stand up, if you'd be so good."

"Great spot," he repeated, kissing her after she was upright. "Great woman."

The sky was a dazzling blue spotted with cottonball clouds. The Sea of Cortez danced and flashed with sunshine, only a shade or two darker. Andy hung out of the TravelAll's window and gawked, hardly knowing where to look first. San Felipe was a sleepy fishing camp town but it was a town. They had passed a few restaurants, a sprinkling of storefronts and two local hotels.

She begged Charlie to stop, pointing at an ice cream vendor on a bicycle. He snorted but pulled over and he didn't decline the drippy chocolate bar she brought back for him.

"Civilization," he said, licking the back of his hand clean. "It's messy and bad for your teeth."

"The big time," crowed Andy. "Decent cooking and clean sheets."

"Don't expect too much of the Hotel Milagro. Just because they call themselves the miracle hotel, don't believe it! The miracle is that they're still open."

He couldn't dampen her spirits. The Morgans, George and Andy had opted for a night's lodging indoors; Charlie and Bill refused. Charlie cited the unnecessary expense. Bill lounged in the hotel's lobby and offered caustic remarks about the hostelry's quality.

"Two potted palms—one dead—and a wrestling poster from Mexico City does not spell Ritz-Carlton," he declared loudly. "With me, it's the best or nothing."

The deskman handed out keys, a small stack of linen and a roll of toilet tissue to each of the guests.

"I'd rather camp out on the beach with Charlie than make my own bed," drawled Bill.

Andy thought fleetingly of the thorn bushes and the pliers and felt better. "I want a hot bath in something deeper than a washbasin. Right now that sounds like the best and it costs six dollars."

"I'll be in the bar next door," Charlie announced to everyone. "They've got free snacks and almost cold beer, as I recall. Who's with me?"

A cheer went up from five throats, choked with dust and tired of drinking water flavored with disinfectant. The bar was nearly as empty and drab as the Milagro, but they were warmly welcomed and treated to large bowls of tortilla chips, heavily salted, and small bowls of chili salsa, a pepper sauce so hot it should have smoked.

"I can call home tonight from the hotel," George jabbered. "My wife was telling me about the reunion of my Seabees buddies when we got cut off. We get together every other year, you see. Now, Mike, in the Big War, WWII, the Seabees..."

Mike gulped down half a beer in one chug, tears welling out of the corners of his eyes. "This chili stuff could cauterize wounds, I swear. George, I'd love to hear it but I'm planning on walking back up the street. I spotted a place with diving equipment in the window and I think they rent it. You want to go on a shopping spree?"

"You're not going," Ray said without bothering to turn from his conversation with Andy and Charlie. "You're not renting, buying or using any of that junk. We're here to fish some more. The fish swim and paddle around, not us."

It was impossible to miss the nasty tone, an undercurrent of warning, in Ray's voice. Andy raised an inquiring eyebrow at Charlie and got a little shake of his head. He knew but he'd tell her later.

Mike didn't reply to his father; he finished the beer and stood up, throwing money on the scarred and stained wood. George, while describing Okinawa, accompanied him to the bar's entrance.

"Damn him," exclaimed Ray, slapping the bar. "The kid can dive like a dolphin, but it's just a sport, right? A pastime?"

Andy caught the look Mike gave his father: annoyance, boredom, possibly determination.

"He's of age," commented Charlie dryly. "He never was too enthused about accounting. At least he didn't sound like it whenever we talked."

"He talked to you about this?" Ray looked shocked. "Well, I hope you didn't give him your blessing. That's what he's after, y'know. He wants someone to tell him these flaky notions of diving as a business, salvage or treasure hunting, makes sense. I won't."

Charlie sipped his beer and said nothing. Andy tried to remember what Mike had told about himself around the nightly fire. She vaguely recalled his mentioning his certification as a diver and his interest in following the progress of a Key West firm searching for sunken Spanish ships. As usual, her clearest memory was of Ray telling his son to "get to the point."

The older Morgan was certainly talkative himself today. She was hoping for a few quiet minutes with Charlie, but Ray was bending his listener's ear and his own elbow with vigor and vehemence. She could piece together the conflict between Ray and his son without much difficulty. Mike had been harping at his father for several years, eager to get a summer job with a California salvage operation, and test his diving skills. He was always showing Ray articles from diving magazines about investments in treasure-hunting outfits.

Ray was adamant. The schemes were silly, the businesses Mike favored were rip-offs, and his son's consuming passion for aquatics and not accounting was a passing fancy, no more.

"Take me and hunting!" Ray said belligerently. "I love it and I'm great at it. But, it's a sport and relaxation. I don't get confused over a hobby. I don't have a bunch of pipe dreams about stalking game."

"There's damn few ways for a professional hunter to earn a living," Charlie inserted deftly. "But there're quite a few openings under water. If a man's really tops, he can make a nice living."

"Nice living," sniffed Ray. "Coming from you, Charlie, that can mean a spare pair of clean socks and the month running out before your money does."

Andy winced. It rang true but it was mean anyway. She wasn't a financial whiz herself, operating on a shoestring to support her so-called hobby, but Charlie was worse. When he'd told her what the Baja trip and the Yucatán one following theirs would profit him, she was astounded. He wouldn't have that dingy office long at the rate he was going.

"I'm poor but proud," Charlie said lightly. He was frowning, though, and Andy saw the whiteness at the taut corners of his mouth.

Ray went on for a while but got no support from Charlie. In fact, he got no more conversation. Charlie was absorbed in staring into the bottom of his glass, lost in some private world. Finally, Ray took the hint and found a more sympathetic listener in Bill.

Andy slid over to the vacated bar stool, hearing Bill's cynical encouragement. "Talk Mike out of it," Bill counseled. "If everyone quits working at real jobs, there'll be too many bums like me hanging around."

"Penny for your thoughts," said Andy. It was the wrong thing to say, she realized too late.

Charlie scowled at her. "Is that the going rate? Or are you valuing my special brand of thinking?"

"Sorry! Don't be so touchy, Charlie. Ray's upset about Mike. He's liable to spout off or take it out on anyone."

"Yeah," he said morosely, "I'm out of sorts myself."

"Want to talk about anything?" She waited for his refusal, expecting it. Charlie could joke or fight but he didn't like to share the depths of his emotions.

"Dreams," he sighed. "Good dreams and bad ones, too. We've all got them, dreams we don't outgrow and give up on. Ray's too practical to acknowledge his or believe in having one. Mike does. You've got a dream, Andy. You want to find a new comet in the class with Halley's, Kohoutek's...a megacomet, a scientific wonder.''

She hadn't thought Charlie paid much attention to her wistful ramblings. She smiled and nodded yes. "Bill lives in a dream," she said. "All his money makes it easy to play and fantasize.''

"But not to win a dream," Charlie added. "Bill can't stick to anything or work at anything. It's no good when a man's dream is too easy to attain. It makes it meaningless.''

She wanted to draw him out, focus on him, but she was aware that Charlie couldn't be rushed. "What about George?" she asked. Eventually, she thought, we'll get around to you and why your dream is troubling you.

"George has achieved his dream. As soon as he recognizes that, he'll enjoy it. He's entitled to it. He did work he liked all his life, had a nice family and home, put in his effort and time. He told me that this trip was his dream vacation, getting away from retirement and his life, but it's only the break he needs to see what he has waiting for him back home.''

"He's catching on." Andy dropped her hand on top of Charlie's and stroked his knuckles. She felt a surge of affection for him—he had patience and insight when it counted. "After he called home from Sky, he was happier, more relaxed. He says he's going to call again tonight from the hotel.''

Charlie gazed thoughtfully into the dusty mirror above the bar. "Well, George is going to be fine, whether he stays or goes before La Paz. He's been reminded of his dream and what he has. He'll want to leave, I think, and make sure it's there for him.''

She bet Charlie that George would make it down the peninsula. She reasoned that once George knew he didn't want to get away from it all, he could stick with the group, enjoy his outing for what it was worth, and not have to review his life in minute detail.

There was a long pause. Andy asked Charlie if she could treat him to a beer. He was preoccupied once more with the bottom of the empty glass in front of him.

"My dream," he said almost inaudibly, "is weird, I guess. I want to see everything in the world worth seeing. I want to put my foot on every continent and in every country at least once. I don't mean to whip through fourteen countries in two weeks, either. I like to see and smell and taste a new place, put it in my brain and soul somehow. It makes me feel good, richer. I don't need photographs or souvenirs."

She stayed very quiet but gave his hand a little squeeze. It was hard for him to put this feeling into words and tell someone, she sensed. He was used to being laughed at, perhaps, for a dream without an ordinary purpose or profit. There wasn't any money or fame or glory in his secret goal, just an accomplishment for Charlie Wilde.

"I'm going to do it," he went on. "And by the time I've achieved it, I hope there's a ticket available for me on a moon shuttle. I could start on other worlds."

"I'm sure you'll make it," Andy said.

She didn't want to laugh. She was touched by his confidence and felt as intimately bound to him as she had been, physically, in a distant mountain clearing.

"Do you think it's silly? Worthless?" Charlie fixed his piercing eyes on her. "Come on, Pruitt, I'm asking. I already know what Ray, Bill or George would say. Yes, it's dumb. Mike's still a kid, in lots of ways, and he'd think it was swell, a worthy and glamorous ambition. Well, he'd probably want to go along if he could. What do you think?"

She met his stare directly, looking into the depths of his dark, troubled and compelling eyes. He wanted the truth and he wanted something else but she had no clue what it was. "It's not my dream, Charlie, but I think it's great…for you. I believe, with all my heart, that people should pursue their dreams at any cost and to the ends of the earth, if necessary. You're literally going to do exactly that and I hope you can."

He toyed with his glass. He rubbed the stubble on his cheek absentmindedly, as if he missed his beard to tug on. He pushed the glass away.

"Let's take a walk," he suggested suddenly. "It's too pretty to be stuck away in a dark, musty bar."

"Sure," Andy said. "You can't take walls or any kind of confinement long, can you? No houses, no hotels."

"Cages," grunted Charlie. "I hate cages."

They had a nice, inconsequential time on the walk, with lots of talk that any two strangers, newly acquainted, could make. *Sometimes friends, sometimes lovers,* Andy was convinced. The mention of "us" didn't come up while they ambled slowly along the shore. They admired the fishing boats and the day's catch openly, and each other slyly in peripheral glances.

The natives of Baja were not wealthy. They eked out an uncertain living in the most inventive ways Andy had seen. The fishing and subsistence farming was not novel, but she had never encountered some of the other occupations. Boys roamed the more popular campsites to dig up the tin cans she had so laboriously flattened and buried, and they resold every usable bit of metal or plastic. Housewives who sold them fresh eggs for breakfast carefully emptied the eggs into the buyer's bowl to save the intact eggshells; the shells were later filled with confetti and sold for use at fiestas.

The San Felipeans had developed another business she found unique. The tide really went out at San Felipe; there was a twenty-three-foot rise and fall when the tides changed, leaving the sands littered with trawlers and beached fishing skiffs. Unless the owner was willing to wait for the incoming tide to set him afloat, he was either stranded high and dry or he hired a car.

Andy and Charlie hung around the beach, watching a parade of the oldest, creakiest jalopies that could still run being flagged by fishermen. The owner hooked up his sputtering, wheezing car to the boat and towed it down to the water's edge to refloat it.

"A car buff would have a field day here," giggled Andy. "Look at that one! Where does someone get a '48 Buick? Is that a Model T?"

"I think they import the leftovers from demolition derbies," Charlie guessed. "Or they send scouts along some of those roads we covered and haul back the abandoned cars."

A shout from a beached trawler attracted her attention. "*Estrellita!* Little star!" a man kept shouting until she returned his greeting.

"It's the shrimper I talked to at Laguna Hanson. Can you imagine? He remembered me."

The captain swung over the side of his stranded vessel and climbed down. Charlie appeared to be amused.

"I can't believe it! He remembered a blonde nearly six feet tall who chases stars down a continent. See if you can use your charm and influence to buy a kilo of shrimp for less than two dollars. That's all I've got in my pocket."

Señor Mondragon loped over and shook Andy's hand, introducing himself to Charlie. He was an instant one man Chamber of Commerce, telling them everything and anything about the town. He wanted to throw in a bonus of a day out on the Sea of Cortez with his shrimper.

Andy had no trouble with Mondragon's Spanish, but the conversation resembled Alice's tea party in Wonderland. The captain spoke in Spanish and while she was chatting, scribbling down the boat's name and time of high tides, Charlie was detailing the smells, the heat, the cramped conditions on board in English.

"I'll tell the men I'm traveling with tonight," bubbled Andy.

"Yes, they must sail with us," the captain insisted. "It will be the highlight of your visit."

"Ray gets seasick, I guarantee you," muttered Charlie. "Bill won't go for a cruise unless he gets an outside stateroom. Ask the captain if his electric winching system needs renovation; George will fix it for nothing."

"What? *Que?*" Señor Mondragon kept asking, wanting a translation and getting none from Andy.

Andy thanked the captain profusely and said they'd let him know how many would accept his hospitality before dawn.

"I'm allergic to diesel fumes," Charlie alibied, pumping the captain's hand in hearty farewell. He clutched the huge paper sack of shrimp Andy had been given as a gift by one of the crew. "Tell him I get hives or I'd go. On second thought, if you go alone, Pruitt, you'll probably come back owning shares in the trawler and with six marriage proposals."

"We do have extra days . . . and nights," Andy reminded him. "As long as I got cheated out of my mountain plans, I'm going to stump for a rest stop and a sea voyage right here."

Charlie knew when he was defeated. "We'll all stay, and anyone with a strong stomach will go."

Eight

They had covered the length of San Felipe once, not that it was much of a feat.

"I'm headed back to the hotel," Andy said finally. "Where are you planning to camp? There was a nice stretch of dunes we passed."

He nodded and gave her a guarded look. "I could meet you for dinner later. Dutch treat, of course."

The Milagro wasn't much, but she pictured Charlie as he stood before her, grimy, gritty and disreputable looking, joining her for dinner.

"I'd like your company," she said, "but you might reconsider taking a room, Chuckles. There's such a thing as carrying this pioneer image too far. What have you got against a bath and a nice, if somewhat narrow, bed with sheets and genuine mattress?"

"Nothing." He grabbed her without warning and gave her a lengthy, languid kiss that astonished a passing fisherman. His fingers tapped out a small sexy message in his own Morse code on her back and sides. "I've wanted you and needed you" was abundantly clear.

"Oh, my," exclaimed Andy when she could talk. "Charlie, don't do that! You make me go flummery inside."

"What?" He laughed at her vocabulary.

"Like custard," she squealed before he did it again. She came up for air, vague and confused. "Does this mean you are taking a room?"

"Yes, and a bath. *Your* room…and a scrubbing with *you*. I would just love to soap your back and every nook and cranny I can reach," he muttered into her ear. "Say yes, please. I can't keep my hands off you, so you might as well put them to some good purpose."

"It's a skinny bed," she teased, feeling her pulse rate pick up alarmingly. "It's a short, old cast-iron tub."

"So much the better," Charlie said. "I have no intention of staying far away from you, Andromeda, if you let me get close."

She was astonished at the variety and intensity of excited images Charlie evoked in her. For a lady of limited experience, she delighted in her own inventiveness and blossoming sensuality. A few suggestions buzzed back into Charlie's ear elevated his heart rate, as well.

She backed away before he could act on them in public. "In an hour," she said, "and don't forget your shampoo. Best bib and tucker for dinner at seven."

"I wish they had room service," Charlie hollered after her. "I bet we don't hit the dining room before nine."

"Any stakes?" she called.

"The usual. Anything you want," he said.

"You're on."

Hot-tubbing, Baja-style, was quite different from the popular California version. The cast-iron tub with claw feet was not designed for a couple, unless they were Pygmies. Andy stepped in cautiously, and the hot water inched higher around her, eliciting sighs of ecstasy. Charlie slipped in and the level rose alarmingly. A miniature tidal wave crested on the curled rim onto the floor tiles.

They heard a waterfall in the distance. The tub's overflow drain connected through the outside wall directly into the street below. The cascade was followed by an angry tirade.

"Whoops, we just gave someone an unexpected shower," Charlie said. Another indistinct but unmistakable Spanish phrase floated upward. "We may be joined momentarily by the management. Wash fast!"

"There's no room in here for the manager. Charlie, where's my washcloth?"

"Find it," he dared her. Her hands dipped and searched diligently. "Not there, but you're on the right track."

While she danced her fingers along his slick wet skin and played with the swirling curls of hair on his legs and chest, Charlie created a soapy bikini top for her. Thus attired, Andy felt inspired to wash his hair, creating giant rooster combs and beards for both of them out of suds. They got the giggles, shushed each other like naughty children and laughed louder.

The bath might have lasted much longer than the hot water did but there was less room in the tub to maneuver than in a rock crevice or a pup tent. Their play was also having more than a cleansing effect. It wasn't the thin mists of steam that made Andy flush and find it hard to breathe.

"When there's more water outside the tub than inside, it's time to quit," Charlie suggested in a harsh, tight-throated way. "I better dry you off, too."

For once, she was in complete agreement with him. It took Charlie as long to rub her dry as to wash her, but she wasn't complaining. He spent too much time on some places and never bothered to get to her feet, but she really didn't care. For every spot he dried, he applied a kiss and the kisses became longer, more ardent and moist. Perhaps it was pointless for him to stroke her lovingly from knee to navel and then follow the path of the towel with his lips and tongue, but Andy was past objecting.

"I must be very tired," she said, holding onto him for support. "I can barely stand up, Charlie."

"Go ahead. Get in bed," he whispered and nibbled lightly on her hip. "I'll take care of certain details. I'll take care of everything if you let me."

She left him searching his pants, soaked and discarded on the tiles. Her skin was impossibly sensitive, charged with the electricity of touching and being touched. When she slid between the coarse, starchy sheets, it was no surprise to see the faint flash of blue sparks. She felt the sparks inside as well, eager and leaping, waiting to join in the lightning they could produce together.

The mattress dipped into a deep valley at Charlie's weight when he joined her. The antique, battered wood of the bed squeaked a warning. There was scarcely space to arrange themselves side by side on the narrow mattress, but Charlie molded her as tightly as he could to himself. Their legs formed a braid, winding and warm.

"You don't have to worry," Charlie murmured in her ear. He brought her hand down along his body and held it to him. "I don't want anything but what's good for you, honey."

"You're good for me, Charlie," she said, parting her thighs and moving gently against him.

His hips, fitted firmly on hers, began to rock in an inviting rhythm. The bed's ancient springs creaked alarmingly in a metallic echo of his every motion.

"We're liable to destroy furniture," he warned. "People will be pounding on the door demanding to know what's going on."

"They'll figure it out," Andy promised. "I don't want to stop. Do you?"

"I couldn't stop if I tried," he said urgently. His hands cupped the mound between her legs, his fingers teasing at her, finding her damp again but with wanting now. "No, I want to start."

And she couldn't wait. They did not have to play anymore. Her knees flexed open, and her hips twisted to sway under his, to rise and fall slightly in anticipation. She felt his hands glide under her, lifting and gripping her hard, and the need for him made her reach to guide his flesh into hers.

Immediately and completely, his thrust joined them and she heard the sound they both made, a low cry from deep within Charlie mingling with an explosive gasp from her. It was a good sound, harmonious and sweet, and louder than any old bed's groaning protest. He moved again, and Andy stayed welded to him, following each long, rippling wave of feeling. There were no words to express such closeness and longing, only sounds and motions. Soft sounds, slow motions.

Charlie strained to arch himself away from her. The muscles along his back and legs quivered, the tendons in his arms stood out in high relief. "Oh, Andy, don't move," he begged. "I don't think I can . . ."

She wanted to tell him not to try to wait, feeling the sharp, almost painful sensations swelling in her. She was with him, in every way imaginable but her mouth was too dry to speak.

His eyes searched her face in a look as tender as his body was hard. Her hands curved around to press the small of his back down to her, her hips lifting to fill herself to overflowing. She allowed another part of her to rise, an ageless, unrestrained womanhood that had power over both of them. She arched and writhed beneath him, setting it free.

"Now," she rasped. "Yes, now."

It was surrender, complete surrender, but she lost nothing by it. Charlie's body lunged, surged on her over and over without restraint.

Her whole being quaked with the force and fury of release. She was reaching to hold him with every cell and fiber, catching him in the intense, seemingly endless spasms that shook her. She felt his body gather strength from her and seek more and more of her, deeper and faster, until he was unable to stop, falling over the brink of his own climax. She gave a very soft, very small cry of jubilance, celebrating them both.

Charlie said in her ear, "I love you." Very distinctly.

His weight settled on her, relaxed and heavy, and his skin felt damp and smooth. He wanted to move away, but Andy wouldn't let him, preferring the comfort of cuddling to more space or air. He tickled the soles of her feet with his toes; she retaliated by scratching along his ribs until he squirmed.

The small room became very quiet when their breathing eased. The rustle of curtains at the open window was audible. They listened to the street sounds and the fainter noises of the sea and the night birds.

"We did it," Charlie groaned, lifting his head and looking around the room. "We broke the bed."

She raised herself on her elbows to peer over his shoulder. Somehow they had fallen considerably below the level of the bed's footboard. Rolling her eyes upward, she smothered some bawdy laughter with her hand at the angle of the headboard.

"I thought you were only joking before," she said finally. "Oh, Charlie, you are quite a man, unsafe at any speed."

"You're quite a woman," he retorted, nibbling her neck and pressing the pillow down over their heads to muffle her sounds. "You made me crazy. It's all your fault for smelling like lemons, tasting like fresh bread... hair like butter... mmmm."

His voice trailed off, his mouth moved downward.

"You must be hungry," whispered Andy. "Let's go get some dinner."

"Not yet," insisted Charlie. "There's plenty of time and lots of you I haven't tasted yet. God, you are a feast of woman."

Their precarious balance on the tilted frame and sunken mattress was not improved when Charlie suddenly shifted to roll her on top of him. He gently rocked her side to side and made little throaty sounds of contentment. More springs creaked ominously and wood fibers splintered and cracked.

"You know everything about me," Andy said. She stroked a rough patch on his chin he'd missed shaving. "Nearly everything," she corrected. "I have operated on the principle of 'take me or leave me' and there haven't been many takers. I put off potential friends and lovers but until this trip, I always thought it was their inability to accept me as I am that screwed up my social and emotional life. It isn't. I was scared to care about anyone too much, positive that they would leave... like Lawton always did. And my mother. And the stepfamilies that followed her. I've kept people at a distance."

"I'm leaving," Charlie said quietly. "You knew that before we got involved. I meant it when I said I love you, but it doesn't change my dream for my life. I didn't want...I don't want to hurt you."

"You haven't," she assured him. "I've hurt myself by being remote, aloof and scared. There's never any guarantees and I wanted one. With you, Charlie, there weren't any games, any guessing; I knew we'd have this time and no more, and still I want it. I want you. Close."

"Me, too." He pressed her head down onto his chest and held it there. His heart was steady and strong, his hands soothing and gentle on her. "We're so much alike, Andy. No, don't snicker. I feel it strongly. We've gone our own way, done our own thing, as people are fond of saying, and we found out we're really out of step with the world at large. We're alone, and the world is big."

"We sure connected," she said with a smile.

"Birds of a feather should flock together." He bounced up and down slightly, flapping his arms unself-consciously and doing his bird whistles. "Even cuckoos need other cuckoos."

Andy put his arms firmly back around her. "Behave, Charlie. We'll end up crashing through the floor, too, and be in the dining room, whether we like it or not, naked as jaybirds."

"And won't they love our attire?" He roared with delight.

She quieted him with a kiss and then another. There was nothing halfway about Charles Wilde, as he himself boasted. The pressure of their mouths grew more insistent suddenly and his hands became daring, roaming her at will.

"Already?" she asked, amazed to feel him stir with renewed virility. "This bed will not go another round. Charlie, I thought you were hungry...."

"I am," he whispered, grinding his body under hers. "But not for food, not yet. And stop thinking…right now."

She took that order happily. Out in the wilds, Charlie was almost always right. In civilized, social settings, however, he had things to learn, manners to polish, and a bet to pay off. He had wagered they wouldn't make the dining room by nine.

Andy was fairly sure she blushed when she told him how handsome he was, how great a lover he was, when she was able to think clearly again. They had a lovely candlelit dinner of refried beans and a delicately broiled marlin steak at midnight. She was positive he blushed when she told him how she'd have to settle the bet. But, he fibbed wonderfully, he was hot under the collar because he'd miss his dessert tonight and flustered by the prospect of having to face the desk clerk with his beady eyes at breakfast.

Early the next morning, there was a brief and unanimous meeting of minds in the Milagro's lobby. Everyone had his own reasons for wanting to spend the extra days left from their premature departure from San Pedro Martir here in San Felipe. Andy's worry that she was the only one luxuriating in the town's meager comforts was groundless.

"I met someone last night," Bill confided. "A very interesting someone. I'd like to stick around and see what develops."

Charlie stopped gobbling at the desk clerk in his broken Spanish and asked Andy to take over. It was vital, he felt, to conduct the explanation of how a bed mysteriously collapsed and bargain over the charges in the man's native language.

"Fooling around is not a good idea," Charlie said to Bill. "It's downright dangerous in Mexico, more so than in lots of other countries. This isn't Paris, Rome or New York, Casanova."

"This is none of your business," Bill shot back. "This is personal."

"A woman!" exclaimed Andy, trying not to miss a word of their conversation while maintaining one with the clerk. "No, I did not ruin an heirloom bed, *señor*. I saw the department store's name stamped on the wood."

"When her family or her children, depending on her age, come after you," Charlie was saying, "you won't have to worry about boredom anymore. You will end up running for your life."

"I could use lots more excitement and exercise," drawled Bill. He gave them all a knowing look and swaggered off across the lobby.

Andy scratched through the figure the hotel man had written down and expressed horror. "A hundred and ten dollars for a bed older than I am? Who is this lady, Charlie? Is she married?"

"I don't know. I don't know," he said dully, following Wiggins's retreating back with hooded eyes. "Well, okay, Bill is on his own, dying to find trouble. What's everyone else got planned?"

Ray and Mike were content to surf cast for the giant totuava, a difficult game fish to catch and fabulous eating. Ray declined Andy's offer of the shrimper voyage, but Mike accepted for the following morning at high tide.

"You didn't intend to hang around here all day and call home, George," teased Andy. "There must be something for you to fiddle around, fix or putter with, or you wouldn't have cheerfully agreed to stay."

"Dune buggies," George said unexpectedly.

The fine white sands of the dunes drew native and visitors alike for racing, but George didn't seem like the usual thrill-seeker. Charlie and Andy had walked along the margins of the dunes yesterday to appreciate the apricot mallow and desert lilies in bloom. They had turned back, discouraged by the roar of the small powerful machines, madly careening up and over hills, and the blue haze of exhaust fumes.

"How about eighty dollars American?" the desk clerk said, tapping Andy on the shoulder. "My final and best offer. You can have a double with a steel frame bed, same rate."

"Done," she agreed, more interested in George's newfound passion. "Here's my forty in pesos. Charlie, please pay the gentleman."

He had stumbled onto the race course by accident, George related. He'd only offered to assist one of the locals with some wiring, on a whim, but stayed the rest of the day, cheered on as a driver.

"I'm not too old. It isn't over for me yet," George said with glee. "And I'm going back today to drive some more. Maybe I'll go on your trawler and maybe I won't. I can't wait to tell Lois about this and show her the Polaroids some guy took of me in that buggy I fixed."

"Muy hombre," snickered the desk clerk. He reached over and shook Charlie's hand, pocketing the other forty dollars. *"Muy, muy, hombre."*

"They are awfully friendly here," said George innocently. "Unless, of course, he wants a bigger tip."

"He said Charlie was quite a man," Andy translated with a perfectly deadpan face. "Very much a man. The clerk might want a few tips but not in pesos. It's a private joke, George."

"I could have bought a damned fine pair of boots with forty dollars," Charlie complained. His cheeks and throat looked distinctly pink to Andy, and he turned away when he saw her scrutinizing him. He didn't complain too loudly or long, either, she noticed.

"You're welcome to come and cheer me on today," said George brightly. "Hey, Andy, you didn't say what you're up to."

"Swim, sleep, and see how some of my photographs turned out," she said. "Halley's visit isn't over yet. I may not win prizes with them but I'm going to fill a huge album of comet snapshots and bore everyone back at PPI to death with my version of what I did on spring break."

"Charlie?"

The chorus of three men's voices were raised to invite him along, inquiring whether he liked the Morgans' plan of surfcasting or rooting for George in a mechanized tin can. Andy studied the scuffed toes of her boots and affected an air of disinterest. She didn't want to hear Charlie lie outright about them spending the day together; it certainly boded better for this relationship if he could be as natural and open about them as he was about everything else.

"How about it, Wilde? What's it gonna be?" asked Ray. "Hurry up! We haven't got all day."

"I do," said Charlie quietly but with an irrepressible grin. "I intend to dog the gorgeous Ms. Pruitt's footsteps today, exclaim over her pictures, carry her bags if she shops, and keep any oglers away from her at the beach. Sounds like my best offer."

"Sounds pretty tame for you, Charlie," chortled George.

"You don't know Andromeda as well as I do," Charlie said. "I'm taking my life into my hands. Of course, some risk is well worth it."

That was all he said, and the mens' reaction was negligible. Ray and Mike nodded and headed for the beach with a brisk, almost military step. George smiled back and hitched his baggy green pants up.

"Buy me a belt, size forty, if you think of it," he instructed Andy. "I'll pay you back. I never have to shop for myself or walk around like a hobo at home; Lois is always looking out for me. I didn't realize how nice it is to have someone take care of you. Make sure Charlie buys you a decent lunch, too. You've lost a couple of pounds since we left, Pruitt."

"I did?" She looked at Charlie for confirmation and got a negative shake of his head. George was off and running, still clutching his waistband in one hand and holding his cap on with the other.

"That was George's way of telling me to do right, man-to-man," Charlie interpreted. "He probably talks to his son-in-law in the same style. You know, the old father-daughter routine where your father says you look thin or you look pale, and he means the man in your life isn't taking his position seriously, watching out for a weaker female's welfare."

"I don't know that routine," Andy sneered. "Lawton was never a doting protective father, and such subtleties only appeared in his scientific papers."

"Maybe that's why you aren't particularly weak," chuckled Charlie. "How about you buying lunch? I just bought half a bed."

"Half a bed is better than none," she said, wrinkling her nose at him. "You can sit and watch me at lunchtime. Better yet, go catch us both fish with your bare hands. You're *muy hombre*, the man said, and here's another chance to prove it."

Charlie bared his teeth and growled at her, making a lunge and missing completely.

Their day was great; the night was even better. Her sample rolls of film were, not surprisingly, everything she had kept her fingers crossed for. San Felipe deserved a gold star, she suggested to the Wilde bunch. But only Charlie and George seemed to share her opinion.

On the predawn walk to Mondragon's shrimper, Bill was jumping at shadows and muttering nonsense to himself. Charlie and Andy shared a conspiracy of whispers at his behavior. Whoever Bill's mysterious lady was, she wasn't doing his mental health any good.

"It'll take so many pills for motion sickness to ease me aboard, I might as well fall asleep on the sand and save myself the trouble," said Ray. He and Mike were giving each other a wide berth, talking through each other this morning.

"Mike must have hooked an elephant shark yesterday," Andy guessed. "Ray's usually this petulant only when someone has caught more snipe or bagged a bigger jackalope."

"The times are changing," Charlie said cryptically. "Strong winds are blowing up between those two."

"Land, sea and air," crowed George at the sight of the trawler. He gave both Mike and Andy hearty slaps on the back. "I'm doing it right on this trip, just like I said I would. Do you think Lois and my neighbors will have me committed if I start building my own dune buggy from the ground up when I get back? Boy, I'd love to... I've got some aerodynamic twists in mind...I can see it. I'll paint it white and gray, to go with my hair, and call it the Silver Fox. Get it?"

Bill Wiggins smiled thinly. "You better plan on a pink leather top, too, then, for your bald spot, Polachek."

Before Andy could unleash her own caustic comment, Mike spoke out. "Aw, dry up and blow away," he said. "I think it's a neat idea, George. There's no age limit or rule about taking up a new interest." He gave his father, not Bill, a stern glance. "There's no IQ cutoff or minimum bank balance required to be a wet blanket, for that matter."

"So sorry," Bill said in his exaggerated manner, unperturbed.

Andy could see Ray was annoyed, however. A storm was brewing in San Felipe with the Morgans, although the real horizon was unblemished with a single cloud. She hated the possibility that anything would spoil the group's last day here, but her feeble attempts at humor fell flat. Ray was the only one staying behind while they all went shrimping; and he was determined to get in a parting shot or two to accompany them in his absence.

"Dune buggying is an unusual and rather unproductive sport at your age, George," Ray said pompously. He returned Mike's defiant stare briefly. "Silly notions are not restricted to any one age group, however. It would be wiser to come back in the boat, not under it, Michael, or swimming in its wake like a demented dolphin."

Mike swore but largely to himself as he waded out and climbed up Mondragon's rope ladder. George shuffled after him, puzzling over Ray's terse judgment. The older man was obviously bothered, constantly fixing his baseball cap once he got aboard, and his eyes stayed focused on the receding shoreline as they floated free.

"Dad is disappointed, for a change," said Mike with bitterness. "He pegged George as a standup, regular guy of his own conservative stripe. It messes my father up to find out people won't entirely conform to their optimum operating standards, as he sees them."

"Your father doesn't know me, then," said George after a minute. "When we were younger, Lois and I were always ready to take on the world, try on new schemes and ideas for size. We used to talk about all the trips we'd take, sports we'd find interesting...." He did another adjustment of his Padres cap, concentrating. "Maybe most newlyweds do that and their ambitions slip by or get cut down to size by everyday life. Well, we had to think of a house and car and kids but we would still talk about what we'd like to do."

Charlie was bobbing his head in sage agreement as if he were telling this tale, not George. Andy recognized his worst fear, the nameless one. It wasn't merely walls and cities and paved roads that made Charlie feel confined and closed in; the demands of a conventional life would ruin him, drain his energy and drive, and kill his dream.

"Lois has been saying how we married for better or worse, but not for lunch," George rambled on. Everyone at the rail laughed, imagining how his poor wife had been forced to listen to rehashed, repetitious stories during the months of George's self-imposed idleness. "She might love a dune buggy. Lois always did like to speed a bit much on the freeways and she's a better driver, too. To heck with my neighbors. They're stodgy blowhards, like Ray Morgan, begging your pardon, Mike."

"Not my pardon," said Mike coldly. "Not necessary."

"It sounds like George found a new spark to relight old dreams," Andy said to Charlie. She supposed Lois Polachek, sight unseen, would heartily approve any kind of rebuilding their castles in the air.

Charlie lifted her hand to kiss its sun-warmed back. "Dear lady, you have uncovered another bonus of every Wilde 'N Free tour. I guarantee you will find yourself as you find adventure. It happens all the time."

"I didn't start out 'lost,'" she said. "And I recall a certain old scout who didn't know his way any too—"

Charlie promptly clamped his hand over her mouth, lest she regale everyone with their rainy night on Juarez Mountain.

"I call it the 'Wilde Effect,'" he said over her mumbles. The basis of his excellent reputation, Charlie continued, was that no one who traveled with him returned unchanged.

Tourists who were forced to take an active part in the world they were experiencing weren't the same afterward. Andy gnawed at his palm until he released her.

"You're a natural philosopher," she gasped. "Also, it's true. Something has happened to us since we left San Diego. We're not the same six people."

"We're only five, for one thing. Wilde doesn't count himself. I'm sure the stench of shellfish is rapidly going to make it four," said Bill. He hung on to the rough rail and looked greenish.

"Oh, the Wilde effect gets more obvious," Charlie said wickedly. The confidence in his voice used to make Andy's teeth grind but she found it funny now. "I can't say how long it lasts because I don't follow up on my clients unless they come back to me for a refresher. But it works, and I do count myself. You can get back to an essential part of yourself by getting back to basics. Any Wilde tour strips off the overlay of complex and complicated problems. You have my word."

"I should have taken my chances with her brothers on shore," groaned Bill, stumbling farther down the railing.

"I'll call Lois from our next stop," George said unrelentingly. "She's sick and tired of me underfoot and unhappy. I'll see what she says."

"Go for it," Mike counseled, but it wasn't clear if he was talking to George alone.

"You made a lovely speech," said Andy, kissing Charlie and promptly biting his earlobe in retaliation. "I was listening, even if no one else was."

The winches began to squeal horribly, and every gust of breeze was saturated with the smell from the nets being lowered. Andy and Charlie hugged each other as if they were sailing on the *Queen Elizabeth*, enjoying this basic reality for all it was worth.

Nine

They were stopping in places that had no name, beautiful sites that appeared on no maps. Dinner meant allowing an hour for fishing and taking the sea's plat du jour. Nighttime meant the stars at every beach and bluff for Andy but more often than not, Charlie came out with her.

Sometimes he counted the meteors or let her show him the special dim and distant places they could never visit. Usually before the night was over he persuaded her to spend a few starry-eyed hours in his arms. She felt she was learning more about heaven than she had thought possible.

Charlie clapped his hands with an excess of morning cheerfulness and whistled sharply through his front teeth. "Are we ready to roll?"

Andy made a mad dash up the street from the bakery. It was a *panaderia* everyone in the last hundred miles had mentioned and she had to try. She heard the tail end of Charlie's whistle and raced along the vehicles in their caravan, distributing sweet rolls filled with guava, crusty pastries, and cocoa-flavored bread. They had sixty miles to do without a stop.

"Ray and Mike aren't talking any more," she panted. "They just glare at each other. I came up behind Bill unexpectedly and he nearly passed out. The Wilde effect is not only more obvious, my captain; it is getting stronger the farther south we go."

"This has been quite a weird week. It must be the comet's influence," Charlie said without fear of contradiction. He puckered up and blew his shrill signal once more before starting the lead car. "I may have to include this group in my memoirs. Everyone but you started out so ordinary, I didn't think they could get this crazy."

"We're falling apart and you're deciding whether or not we deserve a page or paragraph in your future travel book," Andy groaned. She finished her sweet roll and wished aloud for another one.

"Take mine," Charlie offered generously, noticing it was half gone before he finished making the offer. "Trouble and excitement whets your appetite, eh?"

Andy nodded, absorbed in the scenery and taking pictures from the moving TravelAll. A week away from San Felipe was enough to make a firm believer of her in the Wilde effect. What seemed uncharacteristic behavior a few hundred miles up the coast had become acceptable and expected. No one was quite the same.

Bill Wiggins was no longer lazy, bored or self-complacent. He had outdone Ray for speed and efficiency leaving San Felipe, skulking nervously around them and hurrying the others up. His brief but nerve-racking romance with the unknown mystery woman had given him a consuming passion for putting as many miles as possible between himself and her three brothers. Bill, who normally couldn't be whipped into doing more than baiting his own hook, was more than willing to do anything to speed up the journey.

George, on the other end of the human spectrum, was having the time of his life. He talked just as much, but no one objected because his daily enthusiasms were contagious. He bought pottery from Indians along the roadside, as well as wood carvings, saddle blankets and shell jewelry. He helped a rancher construct an ingenious windmill from old auto parts, and acted like a teenager at a Gulf town fiesta they happened on below San Felipe.

"Now that we're getting along, are Ray and Mike going to take up the slack and fight the rest of the way to La Paz?" Andy asked as they picked up speed.

"As long as we stick near water, they will," said Charlie. "Mike went diving for scallops yesterday afternoon. He came back after you went telescoping, I guess. Ray lost his cool when Mike flashed a little wad of pesos he had made selling the extra scallops to another tourist. Morgan said it was dangerous and dumb to dive in unfamiliar waters, and, catch this—*demeaning* to peddle fish like a local. More hasty words and long nasty looks were passed. Mike's got seawater in his veins and Ray doesn't like it."

"I hope their family spat doesn't get out of hand," said Andy. She put her camera away and tried to snuggle her head on Charlie's shoulder. It wasn't easy to be lovers on a washboard dirt road as dusty as a sawmill, but they managed. "It's getting prettier and prettier as we go south. I loved Santa Rosalia; it looked like a stage set for an old Western. And I'm glad you talked us into a day's hike at Mulege to see the cave paintings. I don't want anything to spoil the trip!"

"Hey, if you and I didn't scare the rest of the group off with our major ranting and raving at the start, how can their minor bickering stop the wagon train?"

"It can't. My turn to drive," announced Andy. "You should pull over and let me behind the wheel."

"Not now," Charlie growled. "I saw the fruit stands, too, Pruitt. If we stop and buy mangoes and sugarcane for you to chew on every time—"

"Look in the rearview mirror," Andy interrupted. "George is waving and pointing that way, too. There must be handmade toys or ceramics there for him to look at."

"We'll never make La Paz at this rate!" Charlie shouted out his side. "A hundred miles before dinner. You all agreed!"

"They stopped," Andy said huffily, glancing in the mirror on her side. "I hope George buys me a papaya. Honestly, Charlie, you are the tyrant of the open road."

On and on, the two of them kept at a cheerful sniping while the miles crept by under the tires. The comments got sharp occasionally and their voices got loud, but there were no hard feelings at the end of the day's driving. Their squawking was part of the fun, Andy had decided, and there was never any real venom in the stings they traded, no argument that didn't end with a kiss and a joke.

"We'll be in Loreto tomorrow," Charlie said. "Can La Paz and the Cape be far behind?"

"No," answered Andy, feeling a twinge of sadness. She surveyed their camping site on the open beach and knew she needed to be alone. La Paz meant peace, but she was feeling anything but peaceful this evening. "I'm going to stroll in the dunes. Whistle when George has dinner done, will you?"

"Sure thing." Charlie pinched her butt as she walked by and must have wondered when he got no reaction, no insult. "Hey, are you still angry about that crack I made about your father?"

She had to laugh. "No, Wilde. My father does have the political acumen of a Martian although his ecology views are very sound, because they're in line with yours. I need to be by myself."

"Is that a hint you don't want a companion for viewing meteors tonight?" He looked worried, his brow knit.

"It is not," she said. "I'm trying to get away before you discover I may have left the sand anchors for the tent behind."

She took off, running across the heavily pebbled beach into the relative safety of the sand and surrounding rock hills. Solitude was necessary to sort out the ambivalence she was confronted with. The wind and sea could not entirely erase the sound of Charlie's raised voice following her.

There were not many more evenings like this left and the thought was intolerable. The closer they drew to the Cape of Baja, the nearer she was to flying home, mission accomplished. Shortly, the comet would be forgotten for nearly three-quarters of a century, Charlie Wilde would be in Yucatán, and she would be wanting and watching for her impossible dream. She wished she could assess the Wilde effect on herself.

As she came up a small rise, Andy stopped to see the darting shore birds writing out the random patterns of bird hieroglyphics with their tiny feet. She stayed in the shadows of wind-stunted trees, noticing Mike and Ray only when they frightened the birds and her.

The birds fled. She didn't, although eavesdropping added to her general uneasiness.

It was a little like watching a man argue with himself. Mike resembled Ray so much, even to the angry gestures he made and the pitch of his voice. They stood on the beach a few feet apart with their bodies canted forward to the same degree, their chins thrust out at the same angle. In the haze of dusk, the difference in years was blurred, and the sight of this mirror image struck Andy harder than anything they were saying.

"It's hare-brained," Ray shouted. "Throw away a college education, go ahead!"

"It's what I want to do... what I've always wanted and you damned well know it. Three summers ago, I was ready for Florida, ready and packed."

"To dive with some clown who thinks he can pick gold up off the floor of the sea! Sure, he'd already wasted more than ten years of his life on sunken Spanish ships he couldn't find. Son, there are better, faster and much surer methods to finding a fortune."

"And you know them all," roared Mike. "You know everything, Dad, if I believed your own advertising, You know how to streamline and speed up production. You know how to brag, mostly."

"I produce. I get what I go after," Ray snarled. "You'll end up with a case of the bends and a handful of seaweed, kid."

"I'll end up with my dream," Mike countered. "Mine, not yours. And that's what I'm after."

Ray got livid with rage. He menaced Mike with a fist but didn't touch him. Mike paled under his tan and stood firm, their faces scant inches apart.

"Pieces of eight," mocked Ray. "Chests of rubies and pearls and a mermaid thrown in for good measure. I can see myself telling your mother, phoning the university and canceling your date with the latest love of your life when I get back. You won't have time to handle those mundane details. You'll be too busy counting your gold."

The younger Morgan pivoted on his heel in the sand and started to walk away. This particular argument had been acted out on several occasions, Andy realized, and Mike was writing an end to the play this time. His jaw was set and his step showed a final determination. Ray had to have the last word, but it was Mike's move. He did not see his father's hand reach after him, but Andy did.

"You'll end up broke," he called. He sounded more like an oracle than an angry father or a man trying to reason with another man. "You'll be a bum, Michael. All bums have a dream and nothing else."

The only indication that Mike heard him was when he walked faster, breaking into a run, sprinting along the beach. The wind licked up the waves and the sea, inching onto the golden sands, erasing his footprints as quickly as he left them.

Andy went down the dunes to stand near Ray. He was still gazing off in the direction Mike had taken. She put her hand on his forearm, wanting to say something and not quite knowing what it was. As soon as Mike disappeared, Ray looked more like a distressed and defeated father. His shoulders were rounded, slumped and his complexion was tinged with gray under his tan.

"What an ambition," he said sadly, more to himself than Andy. "Salvage diver, treasure hunter...bum. He had everything fine going for him. He's everything good I could have asked for in a kid."

She wondered how few times Mike had heard the praise Ray was offering to the thin air.

"He'll be okay, then," she said. "Mike's sharp and very competent for twenty-one. He could succeed at almost anything he sets his sights on."

Ray seemed to notice her presence for the first time. He put his hand over hers and shook his head at her in a disapproving manner. "I sure hope not. God, I hope not. If he fails, he'll come to his senses and head home. If he actually does this stupid thing and sticks to it, what the hell will he be? A deep-sea Charlie Wilde, a footloose and feckless survivor, that's what!''

Andy took her hand back roughly and wanted to unleash a sample of her choicer oil-field vocabulary on Ray. But he was just warming to his subject.

''Worthless ideas and impoverished dreams,'' ranted the older man. ''Like what's-his-name in Florida with his dreams of doubloons! Charlie chasing his tail all over creation, Mike sailing the seven seas. Stupid!''

She could criticize Charlie, at great length, but she didn't like to hear Ray bad-mouth him. She didn't think much of a father who wished failure on his son or acted as if he had the lock on life.

''Ol' what's-his-name found it,'' shouted Andy, ''for your information. Forty million dollars' worth, Mel Fisher and the *Atocha*! And even if he hadn't, it might not have been counted a waste by some people. I'll spend the next ten years searching for a new comet, and if it doesn't show up, I won't count the years as a waste.''

''Then you're as nuts as they are,'' Ray said with unshakable confidence.

And, obviously, she was worth as much attention as his nutty son. Morgan took off at a brisk pace, leaving Andy to swear at the gulls swooping above the shallows.

She sat there for a while, digging her bare toes deep into the sand and sifting handful after handful of the coarse grains through her fingers. The anger cooled, the arguments ended and what was left? Love or nothing?

The scene she'd witnessed was too vivid a reminder of her and Charlie. She didn't want to dwell on it but it nagged at her. Ray and Mike were a close father-son pair; the likeness didn't end at their physical resemblance. She and Charlie could be as solidly and intimately linked, when they were on the same side. There were moments when she felt as if they thought exactly the same way. Those were the best times, hinting to her that there were bonds between them impossible to break. Like Mike and Ray.

She gazed out at the horizon where it met the sea, a beautiful, vast but empty view. Her life before meeting Charlie resembled this scene. There was motion and color and plenty to occupy her, but also a curiously flat quality, a sameness that was punctuated by very few memorable moments: her degree, the comet's discovery, some high and low spots she wouldn't forget.

But the world was different when she was with Charlie, whether they were in concert or disharmony. She felt more alive, more alert, more challenged every second. She felt she wasn't missing a thing, and there were no flat places, only peaks and valleys. She loved him fiercely one minute, hated him utterly the next, and knew—whichever emotion had her in its grip—that it was better than any other time in her life. And it was coming to an end very soon.

She hiked up the beach to the caravan. Ray and Bill were surf-casting while George was napping with a newspaper tented over his head. In front of the propane stove, Charlie was dancing delightedly from one steaming cauldron to another. Shirtless, barefoot and with a ridiculous woven palm hat perched on his head, he dipped into a pot, extracted a rosy shrimp and dropped it a brief curtsy before popping it into his mouth.

"Yummy! My best effort," he crowed. Nobody seemed suitably impressed. He swiveled around and fished out another one for Andy. "Here, pretty lady, this will put a smile on your face."

"And a lily in your hand," mumbled George from beneath his reading material. "Don't trust him, Andy."

"She wants to live dangerously," growled Charlie. "She wouldn't be here if she didn't. Here, Chef Wilde's own recipe for gumbo."

Andy accepted the shrimp against her better judgment to flatter Charlie and ask him, out of George's hearing, if he'd seen Mike.

"I caught a glimpse of him. He came back a few minutes ahead of Ray, scooped up some of his stuff and split," Charlie said casually, apparently unconcerned.

Andy tried to signal him to keep his voice down but, of course, being subtle with Charlie was like waving a flag in front of a bull. "He and Ray had a big fight," Andy whispered. "Did Mike say anything about this quarrel? Or where he's headed?"

Charlie digested her information with a few more samples of his own bubbling creation. "No, I figured they had words from the way Ray acted. Hey, no sweat! Mike either took off to be alone and think out whatever's gnawing at him or he's made his decision and he's left."

"That's pretty cavalier of you," Andy said with a frown. "Don't you care?"

"Yeah, I care," Charlie replied. "I can't do much about it, in the first place. And, in the second, I'm not sure I would if I could. I hate meddlers and people who want to fix other people's problems. I've got my own to handle."

"Well, what do you think?" persisted Andy. "Will he be back?"

He grinned. "Tell me how you rate the gumbo and I'll tell you."

Exasperated, she glared at him. "It's good," she declared grimly. "I mean it. You have a winner there, finally. Now, about Mike? You know more about this than you've let on. I could tell in the bar."

"Mike's gone," Charlie predicted to her. "For good, I'd say. George will be next to leave, probably. We may limp into La Paz like a pair of played-out old prospectors, just you and me."

"You don't sound overly worried," noted Andy, snatching a freshly peeled shrimp out of his bowl. She bit into it hard, as if she were snapping someone's head off. "Do you lose many people on your tours, Charlie, on a regular basis?"

"Always a few deserters," he said with a faint smile. "The weak, the homesick, the ones who are bone lazy and the ones who sass back and get sent packing."

"Which category did Mike fit?" She managed to grab one more shrimp before he blocked her expertly with a football move, shoving his hip into hers. "Ouch!"

He gave her a quick peck on the cheek, checking first to see who else was watching. "Serves you right. Mike wasn't any of those types. He is a special case, striking off to blaze his own trail. I hope it was the two trips he took with me that had something to do with his move. This jaunt may have pushed him right over the edge of this decision. He thought if Wilde can make adventure pay, anyone can."

"You better not let Ray hear you say that," Andy warned. She told him the essence of the scene she'd witnessed and the follow-up with her. "Ray's still pretty hot under the collar and fairly miserable, too. He won't admit it, I'm sure. But he might make trouble if he thought you encouraged Mike to go in any way, shape or form."

Charlie munched on his shrimp while he chewed on the idea, as well. "Mike's a man," he said finally. "He's responsible for his actions, not me. As for Ray and what he thinks, I don't much care. I never duck trouble if it comes to me; I just don't go out looking for it."

"Oh, pooh," Andy commented succinctly. "You do so. What else is all this roughing-it, tough-guy travel about if not trouble? Scars? Fractures? It's not to earn the riches of Peru."

"Ad-ven-ture," Charlie enunciated with exaggerated care. "Love me for the dangers I've passed, not the trouble I've made, darling."

She wrinkled her nose at him and was about to stick out her tongue for good measure when she saw Ray advancing toward them. "Get ready to pass," she advised and wandered over to the coffeepot. She wanted to be near enough to hear and far enough removed to avoid fighting with Ray again.

"I'm sure you know what's happened," Morgan said affably. "I guess I was plenty vocal about Mike's taking off."

"You were," said Charlie.

Ray took a deep breath and let it out in several puffs. "Well, uh, we can assume he won't be back. At least, not for the rest of the trip. He'll be sorry, sooner or later, and go back home, but not for the duration of our arrangement, certainly."

"Get to the point," said Charlie mildly. Andy had to smother her face in her hands and choke down a mouthful of hot liquid, nearly strangling.

Ray reddened. "I'm talking about my refund, Charlie. The boy's gone. There's better than half the trip left and I paid for two up front . . . in full."

"So did everyone else," Charlie said. "That's how I do business. It's nonrefundable once we hit the road unless I cancel or drop dead. I don't even exclude acts of God; I led a terrific group through the Everglades with a hurricane roaring past our ears once. Two of the members scurried up to Miami for cover, and I didn't write them a refund check."

He spoke in a calm, reasonable tone but with such a hint of steel that Andy assumed the discussion was over. When she and Charlie fought, she pictured him getting as worked up as she did, gesticulating, sputtering, cursing. Maybe he was cool because he didn't much care about Ray and what he thought. Charlie was in admirable form now, demonstrating good manners and cogent arguments all over the place.

For one brief second Andy was glad Charlie didn't fight this coldly with her. Proof positive, he cared for her. She had gone around the bend, after all, if she was thinking they fought wildly because they cared recklessly.

"I retain the best lawyer in San Diego," Ray was saying. "The man hasn't lost a case in twenty-two years."

"He's due for a loss, then," said Charlie. "My contract will stand up in court and so will I, if necessary. There's no fine print with me, Morgan. You pay. You go as far as I go if you can."

Ray made a fist and pounded it into the palm of his other hand. The loud smacking sound made Andy start nervously, but Charlie, she noticed, didn't blink. "Mike will be sorry. And so will you, Charlie. So will you."

"Maybe," Charlie said noncommittally and he shrugged. "It wouldn't be the first time." He looked down into his bowl, rummaged for a piece of shrimp and looked up once more, adding, almost as an afterthought, "But don't be so sure about Mike, Ray. It takes guts to follow a rough road when he knows in advance he might not get there. Mike's aware that he picked a really competitive, cutthroat business. A man with his courage and determination won't end up regretting his decision."

"Like hell," Ray spat out. "Come and tell me this same bull when you're twenty years older and not so energetic, your vision not so keen, but your wallet just as skinny."

Andy drew in her breath sharply. Charlie should explode any second, she guessed.

Instead, Charlie chuckled. "I'll put it on my calendar and roller skate over to your nursing home, I promise. And I'll tell you. Or I'll weasel out of it and say that any decisions a man regrets should be his, not yours. Why don't you let Mike make his own mistake, if that's how it turns out? Why don't you pray nonstop that Mike becomes the best salvage diver in the world and gives you something you can justifiably boast about?"

"This has to rank as one of the most bizarre love affairs on record," Andy said. "We will, we won't, we do and we don't. Charlie, watch out for these bushes. They're scratching the paint right off the sides. I wish we took the main road."

The pass along to the Gulf was exactly as wide as a single vehicle and lined with vegetation that behaved hostilely. Andy ducked as a swinging, thorny limb scraped closer, narrowly missing her.

"This *is* the main road and the only pass," Charlie grunted. "It's getting better."

"What? The road or this affair?"

He leaned over, risking collision with a cactus to kiss her. "Both, honey. When we stop at the next service station, I'm planning on strolling down lover's lane with you."

She swatted him with the map, demanding he keep both hands on the wheel. She chortled at his romantic suggestion. "Service station" meant any tiny store or outpost ranch in the peninsula. If Charlie assigned the task of straining gas and filling the five-gallon red cans to someone else, she and he could slip off to cuddle in the midst of spiny chollas or thick-trunked elephant trees with only a snake or desert rat as witness. The appeal of a service station rendezvous was limited, she said prudently.

"If you have high hopes of being romanced by candlelight, wined and dined to strumming guitars, we'd both be clinging to hope alone until we reach La Paz," Charlie reminded her. "Very few honeymooners would pick this trip unless they considered insect bites sensual and sand rash enticing."

Andy shifted uncomfortably in her seat and felt the inward bite of chagrin. They were not honeymooners and she mustn't forget that fact. The limits to their affair were geographic and chronological and already set.

"As you probably guessed by now, dating and marrying were not high priorities for my life. I'd settle for a little privacy away from the group and the time to enjoy it," she said bluntly.

"Too bad," Charlie said offhandedly. "You are not only smart and beautiful, you're impressively patient and compulsive once you get an idea fixed in your head. You'd make a great, although offbeat, mother, Andy."

"I'm sure I will be." She answered without thinking. "In fact, it's all set. In the next five years, I'm determined to have a baby."

Charlie narrowly avoided breaking an axle in a crater that she would have expected to see on the moon. "Run that by me again," he suggested loudly over the engine's roar. "To look at you, Ms. Pruitt, it's hard to tell how flaky you are. It takes two people and nine months to have a baby."

"No, it takes two people to make a baby, generally, but only one has it. And I am not an outstanding flake, thank you. My plan has a logical, sensible and sound basis. I've given it a lot of thought, Charlie."

She probably shouldn't have said anything, thought Andy, but it was too late to retract her statement. Besides,

t was just as well to know all the areas she and Charlie could
ot agree on or discuss without getting riled up. She could
rite an encyclopedia of their disagreements after the trip.

He pulled over abruptly, sending the tires on her side into
he slanting ditch, placing the vehicle in a precarious posi-
ion. He leaned out his side and waved the others on ahead,
iving each driver a thumbs-up sign so no one would bother
o stop and offer help.

"*This*, I have to hear!" he said. "Is there anything con-
entional and ordinary about you, Andromeda?"

"Charlie, do not gawk at me as though I am from an-
ther planet," she requested. "When I get my doctorate, I
ill get a full-time position teaching, with good hours,
enefits and a lovely university environment to raise a child
n. Actually, I took the job at Pacific Polytechnic to help me
with my future maternity plans as well as to give me free
venings for astronomy. I'm reasonably certain they'll of-
er me tenure in another year, when my dissertation is fin-
shed."

"Haven't you left something out?" Charlie asked face-
iously. "A husband? A father? I suppose you have picked
im out of some catalog or star atlas. I seem to recall you
elling me about a terrific yen for security and stability in
our nature."

"Just because I can't find it for myself doesn't mean I
an't provide fully for a child," Andy said. "Don't be so
ld-fashioned, Charlie. There are tons of single parents
owadays. I'd appreciate it if we got back on the road; I'm
etting queasy at this angle."

"Well, it's not morning sickness, at least," quipped
Charlie. He started the engine and hopped the Jeep back
nto the road with more of a bounce than was necessary. "I
must be old-fashioned. I better stay in the woods or out on

an ice floe for the rest of my life." He gunned the motor
rounding the curve like a madman, and said nothing more

The dusty little rancho up ahead qualified as a Baja town
with a sign proclaiming that groceries, bottled water, ga
and tire repairs were available. Charlie nosed the Jeep nex
to the other parked tour vehicles and put a restraining hand
on Andy before she could get out.

"There're some things I want to say," he began so
emnly. "Things I haven't ever told anyone before."

Strain made him look earnest, almost boyish. "Certain
species mate for life and I think I'm, by nature, one of thos
creatures. Now I see how my ideas might strike you as na
ive and antiquated but I'm like an old trumpeter swan. I wa
convinced when I got married that it would be forever."

"Charlie, there's no need to explain yourself to me...I'n
aware that you don't like talking about personal, privat
matters and I accept it. I spoke my mind back there be
cause I wanted to, but you aren't obligated..."

He continued, staring through the grimy windshield and
fiddling with the keys in the ignition. "I followed Jane back
to San Diego. I tried to straighten our marriage out, work
ing there full time for six months. I was miserable and go
fired. Her family and friends found me peculiar; I would
describe them as snobs, chiselers and mooches. I couldn'
beat them and I wouldn't join them, getting soft in the belly
and the head, and so it didn't work."

"I'm so sorry it didn't," Andy heard herself say in a smal
pained voice. She experienced a blinding flash of hatred fo
Jane, sight unseen, and was well aware that she was not un
prejudiced, not being fair.

Charlie was, objectively, no picnic to live with. He coul
be irritating, arrogant, and totally impossible to get along
with in his element. He must have been a beast, a real fish

out of water, stranded in a society setting. But she could see how tortured he was by the failure of his marriage.

"Jane suggested we have children," Charlie said and finally looked at her. "She was every bit as serious, organized and modern about it as you were a few minutes ago. I guess that's why I got so stirred up. Another of my oddball notions is that kids spring from love, not a timetable."

Ray and George came out of the ramshackle store with cans of beer and soda cradled in their arms. Ray headed toward their Jeep, and Andy shook her head in warning to him. She suddenly wanted to hear whatever Charlie would tell her. It was very important—but not to hear his secrets so much as to examine one of her own.

She had always doubted the reality of lasting love, she realized with a kind of horror. She had passed up the company of nice, bland men, telling herself she preferred her solitary, uncomplicated existence to a lukewarm, mediocre love affair. But she had been afraid of discovering there was such a stable but uncontrollable element in herself until Charlie had brought it to light. She didn't believe in what she could not see before, a legacy of the constant shuffle of faces and places in her childhood.

"I did leave," repeated Charlie sadly. "I did run away. Whenever I went back after a trip, I realized we were straying further and further from marriage. Maybe families and couples married for life are nearly extinct species. I'm feeling old, fossilized right now."

"You'll survive," she said, "but I'm thirsty. How about letting a lady buy you a root beer?" She nodded in the direction of the store's wide-planked porch. Charlie followed her gesture, noticing the three men in their party had assembled and were watching them intently.

"How long have we been sitting here?" Charlie asked.

"An hour," said Andy.

Charlie looked at her, clearly embarrassed. "I don't think I ever talked an hour nonstop before today."

"Sure you did," she said with a grin. "In our cave one rainy night. For a flake and fossil, we seem to have lots to say to each other."

He laughed, reaching across her to open her door. "You are a lady, Andromeda—a really fine and classy lady. And I don't care how old-fashioned that word is. Yeah, you certainly can buy me a root beer and show me how liberated you are."

"Not with an audience," teased Andy. "But we'll be in La Paz soon, and civilization has one advantage. Doors! You know, the wooden things that close . . . and lock."

Ten

—

"Nine hundred sixty-seven miles down, twenty to go and our goal in sight!" Charlie made a sweeping gesture with his hand, offering his Wilde bunch their first glimpse of La Paz from a high hilltop. "Gentlemen and lady, the 'pearl of the peninsula' awaits us!"

The pearling industry of Baja's largest city was largely defunct, but La Paz still retained the deserved nickname. Even at this distance, a pale glow appeared to hover around it. White sands and surf, whitewashed buildings and the light-paved streets merged into a shimmering beacon under a near tropical sun.

"If there's one pearl left for sale, Lois is getting it," declared George. He clambered quickly back into his van before anyone could josh him about the impossibility of his fitting another gift item into a steamer trunk, let alone his suitcase.

With Mike's abrupt departure, George had appointed himself sole driver of one of the vehicles, refusing to let any passenger take up the extra space. Empty cereal boxes filled with polished olive shells and conches, keyhole sand dollars and rocks were for his neighbors kids. Ceramic and wooden owls were neatly wrapped in newspapers for his wife's collection, and the entire back seat was heaped with his fat-bellied clay pots and antique shards. A hideous red-and-blue plaster dune buggy occupied the seat next to him in a place of honor.

"I'm glad someone can profit by Mike's absence. I sure haven't," Ray said tensely, referring to the driving arrangement. He took his constant partnering with Bill as an affront, but since Mike left, Ray took offense easily over everything.

"We miss Mike, too," Andy said sympathetically.

"Miss him, hell," was Ray's response. "He cost me money for this trip and more in worry. I meant that! At least he cleared out and gave George room for his junk and knickknacks."

"Come on, Ray," urged Bill, pushing him gently away from the hilltop vista. "We can beat Polachek and those lovebirds to town, and I'll buy you the biggest, coldest drink they've got." It was a rare show of friendly concern from Wiggins, and it worked. Ray quit grousing and talked instead about the size of the marlin he intended to catch.

They left the shadow of the silvery olive trees to follow the smooth banked road to La Paz. Technically, the end of the trip was marked by their arrival in the city. Charlie had booked everyone into a comfortable hotel for two days and nights of rest and recuperation from the grueling month. Their plane tickets back to California were waiting. Bill had wired ahead, naturally, and switched himself to the most luxurious, expensive resort, as well as offering to host a champagne breakfast for the entire group, his parting gift to them.

"Lord Bountiful won't be one of your repeat customers," said Andy, referring to Bill. "He's revving up for some drinking and carousing in an onyx bathtub to celebrate. He's confident that La Paz has exotic women, without brothers lurking in the laurel trees, and the kind of danger he understands best: fast cars, high-stakes gambling, hard liquor."

"No loss," shrugged Charlie. "I feel badly about Ray, though. He's not a half-bad guy, and we've taken a few good trips together. Unless he resolves his feelings about Mike, I'll probably never see him again, either."

"And George?" she asked with a puckish grin. "Do you expect his business for another trip?"

"I'm sure of it," said Charlie, surprising her. "George had the best time of any of us, I think. I'll see him... and Lois real soon. Even I can't always tell at the beginning of a trip who is going to become Wilde 'N Free—but George has."

She couldn't dispute who had the best time in the Baja. Charlie was too busy telling tales of the migrating gray whales bearing their young in Magdalena Bay.

"You ought to come back here some winter," he advised her. "A baby whale is as impressive to see up close as a supernova. Why, we missed as many sights as we saw...."

She wouldn't come back to the Baja, she knew. It wouldn't hold the same fascination for her without the comet, the Wilde bunch, and, above all, Charlie. Halley's was disappearing; her vacation was winding down, as well.

"Many people go traveling all their lives and never realize it wasn't mileage they were after," she said, paraphrasing his favorite quote from Thoreau. "I got what I was after, Charlie. And I'm not complaining."

His eyes, dark amber in the sunlight, sought hers. "Maybe you'll be with me on another trip," he said tentatively.

"Maybe," Andy said without conviction. She didn't have to review all the reasons, there wasn't much chance of it happening. Charlie was aware of her future plans; it was school and work, Waverly Oil and astronomy for her.

The sighting of the first television antenna in a month was a shock to her system, eliciting a small gasp. A sleek silver jet angling down in an ultramodern airport looked odd, not ordinary. They had traveled through time, as well as the space of a thousand miles, in traversing Baja. The Spanish colonial charm surrounding them was overwhelming, otherworldly after the simple, uncluttered peninsula.

The average traveler flew into La Paz, found it an attractive tourist center with a foreign flavor and, without much thought or ado, flew home. There was, Andy mused, a corollary to Charlie's theory of the Wilde effect. After being reduced to basics, his clients viewed the modern conveniences they took for granted with a different eye.

From every side of the scenic waterfront drive, she was bombarded with sights, sounds, and smells that she took for granted in San Diego and now regarded as brand new. A traffic light was as novel as a spiny caterpillar cactus would have been four weeks ago. Glittering walls of glass on a multistory office building reflected coconut palms and the placid blue sweep of the bay; they were something to marvel at, especially when she hadn't glanced in a mirror for weeks.

"It's funny how fast you can forget certain things," she said when Charlie had to circle the block their hotel was on

everal times. "I put the whole idea of traffic jams and
parking problems out of my head completely, as if they
didn't really exist."

"Don't I wish," grumped Charlie. "You hop out and
register us. I'll meet you at seven-thirty for dinner or in the
room for a nightcap, whichever comes first, after I try to
park this heap somewhere."

Andy patted his arm consolingly. "It's almost noon,
Chuckles. I really think you'll manage before then. Trust
me—and don't get so uptight just because you saw a stop
sign and a parking meter. This is vacation land, too, and no
one will make you put on a tie and jacket. We're going to
enjoy today and tomorrow, aren't we?"

The last official gathering of the group was supposed to
take place in the hotel's lobby. Charlie shuffled through
papers and handed out their return tickets, but no one said
goodbye. They milled around, including Bill, hefting their
luggage and discussing individual plans as if actual separa-
tion from the group was too painful to contemplate.

Andy had always presumed the spirit of togetherness took
a long time to develop. Certainly, over the past month, all
of them, singly or en masse, had openly wished for an end
to the trip, griping about the others or the rigors of the
journey. The moment had arrived when they could do anything they wanted, and they stayed clustered in the lobby,
making plans for dinner, as if they were still huddled out in
the desert around a fire. Togetherness hadn't worn thin, it
seemed.

"I'm going to give you our address," George said to her
with a paternal hug. "I want you to come and meet my Lois,
show her your photos and visit with us back home."

"This is like the end of summer camp," Bill said sarcastically. "I'd offer to take you to Paris, Pruitt, but I won't promise to write from there."

She shook hands with him, a mischievous light filling her eyes. "That's okay, Bill. The skies over Europe aren't very good for viewing, anyway. You stay out of thorn bushes, hear?"

Ray was too busy reading something the clerk had handed him to give Bill more than an absentminded nod. Finally he strode across the lobby with a springier step than they'd seen in days. He held up a garishly colored postcard, flicking it impatiently with his thumbnail.

"Where the deuce is Popotla?" he demanded of Charlie. "This was waiting at the desk from Mike. He's there."

"It's on the Pacific side of the peninsula," Charlie said. "Not too far south of the U.S. border. It's a rough and tumble place, a real Barbary Coast town but a diver's haven."

"Mike's got a job." Ray whistled and scanned the card once more. "Listen! He walked into a scuba shop and they hired him to repair and sell their equipment. He's following up a lead on a Mexican salvage firm and will write later."

"That's nice," Andy said very cautiously, not sure what Ray's reaction was going to be. Mike was proving himself the epitome of efficient, direct motion, disproving his father.

Ray smiled at her with evident pride. "That's damned amazing," he said. "Mike doesn't speak much Spanish. He had the clothes on his back, a few bucks in his pocket and he made it clear up and across the whole Baja. How, I'll never know!"

"You'll know," said Charlie. "He's writing, so he's still thinking about you. You'll see him one of these days and find out."

Ray just kept bobbing his head, reading and rereading the card. "And the man already got himself a job! Didn't waste a minute...."

Andy noted Ray's switch from "my boy" a few short weeks ago to "the man." Charlie could kid all he liked about the Wilde effect but it was real. The trip had wrought changes in them, some subtle and some dramatic. Charlie had questioned how long the Wilde effect lasted and had no answers, but she did. Charlie made no claim that Ray was going to keep his son's independence in perspective or George would retain his new lease on life indefinitely. He didn't say that Bill had finally learned that his money was no protection, defense or excuse.

There was one permanent change she knew about. She had gone hunting for a comet and been snared by love. There might be today and tomorrow in sunny La Paz, but deep in the darkest, remotest corners of her heart and mind, Andy was already sure that the Wilde effect was permanent. With or without him, loving Charlie was forever.

"What happened to Andy Pruitt?" Charlie asked. "I asked her out to dinner, not you. I don't know how to act around a movie star."

"Thank you," she said, taking his look and compliment as her due. She couldn't resist another peek at herself in the mirror before they left. Movie star, no. Miracle, yes.

Finding a dress and a pair of shoes was easy. There were shops and boutiques in La Paz crammed full of beautiful and tempting resort wear. She had passed over the imported, less affordable clothes and picked out a brilliant pink cotton dress, hand embroidered with fantastic, fanciful designs. The vivid colors set off her tan and the sun-bleached white gold of her hair.

The most difficult part of getting ready had been whipping herself into shape. A month of hot sun, dry winds, and rugged living made her skin and hair less than lovely. She'd never worked so hard before on herself, slathering on the avocado conditioner the lady in the *farmacia* had recommended, smoothing and oiling and brushing and buffing.

"I made reservations at Jaramillo's but maybe you'd like another place better," Charlie said stiffly. He mentioned the ritziest hotel in town.

Andy shot him a curious sidelong look. "Jaramillo's is fine. But something's already eating you, Charlie. What is it?"

"I should change," he said, stopping dead in the lobby. He rubbed his face with its minor coating of stubble. "I should shave, too. You go have a drink in the bar and I'll be right back."

"Charlie, it's almost nine and my stomach is growling so loud, the lady on the elevator with us thought there was a mechanical problem." She pulled his hand away from his unsmiling face and tugged at his arm.

He wouldn't budge an inch. "I feel funny," he said.

"Sick?" She peered at him anxiously and felt his forehead. He did look flushed and peculiar but he wasn't feverish.

"No, I just...I think it's..." He made a few feeble attempts at explanation and gave up, gesturing weakly with his hands.

The look of consternation on his face and the peculiar circling motions didn't add up for Andy until Charlie had already started to back off. Then she understood and ran after him. Charlie was not clumsy physically unless he was feeling emotionally awkward.

"You don't like me like this," she said, braking him with much effort. "Makeup on, hair done, dressed up. You don't want to change your clothes but you aren't comfortable with me when I'm..."

"Dolled up," supplied Charlie. He smiled sheepishly, and swept her up and down with open appraisal. "It's not exactly that I don't like you this way. I remember how you knocked me out the way you came into my office and how gorgeous you were when we went out for dinner that night. I feel like a jerk, sometimes, when I'm around someone who looks like you do. I got used to seeing you as Andy on the trip, not an awesomely fine beauty."

"Thanks again," she said with a smile. "Getting compliments from you is like pulling stickers, Charlie. I'm still Andy, barefoot, boots or high heels. Don't be silly—and let's go eat! In two minutes, I'll start gnawing on you."

He laughed, and the stiffness left his posture. "What a puny threat, Pruitt! I'd love to be your appetizer."

She nearly slipped and told him he was the main course, the only and most appealing man for her love feast. She didn't, keeping the smile frozen on her face as they marched out, arm in arm. The joke was too close to the truth to make; there was a sharp sting to the thought that tomorrow she would be returning to her normal steady diet of work and school.

If she thought for one second Charlie would ever come back with her, she would ask him to. If he would stay in a city longer than the time it took him to organize another tour, she could imagine living with him, sharing her apartment. She was daydreaming; compromising was a virtue neither of them possessed.

Jaramillo's was crowded with vacationers, but she didn't notice. She forgot what she ordered long before the meal arrived and ate it all without tasting most of it. Charlie was not doing much better, she noted. He dropped his fork twice and fed himself mechanically, never taking his eyes from hers. The waiter had to clear dishes from under their clasped hands.

"It's not quite the same as our first dinner together, is it?" she asked. "You wanted to stick me with your cocktail fork and drown me in the drawn butter."

He ducked his head and laughed softly to himself. "Not quite, Andromeda, but I didn't trust myself to order the flaming dessert. You were the coolest customer I'd encountered in a long time. I think that's really why I kissed you in the parking lot; if I couldn't set you on fire one way, I was willing to try another."

She picked a carnation up to tickle him under the chin, and he snatched it away from her. "And I," she said dreamily, thinking back to a night that seemed a hundred years ago, "I thought you were the roughest, most unpolished and compelling man I'd ever met. Don't ask me if I changed my opinion. Ask me if I'm happy…because I am, Charlie. Wildly happy, if you like puns."

"How can you be happy?" Charlie ripped the pink flower into a heap of perfumed petals and picked at the stem, peeling off the leaves. "It's over. As of tomorrow, we'll be history. I'm flying to Mexico City and you'll already be back in San Diego."

She picked up a handful of the tattered flower and put the silky remnants into her purse. They seemed an appropriate souvenir. Charlie had given her the flower in a traditional romantic gesture and then, before the evening was over, was aggravating her by tearing it apart.

"I'm happy," she repeated. "We knew what was coming and went ahead anyway. It's not as though we can't ever see each other again, Charlie. You know where I live, where I work, and what I'll be doing for the next couple of years. When you're in San Diego, between trips..."

He made one of his horrible animal noises, alarming the people at the next table. "Oh, yeah, I can see it. We meet at the airport or at my office where I happen to be living, in case you didn't know—please God, don't let the rental agent find out! Or we set up a rooftop rendezvous wherever you're parked to stargaze. I'll bring the cooler, you bring the blanket."

She was so sure she could be mature and self-possessed earlier this evening. Getting ready, she was determined that their last night together would be a wonderful memory, a perfect parting without tears and tantrums.

"Buzz off," Andy said stridently. "If we can't discuss these matters like adults, our relationship can't be worth much."

"I am buzzing off," bellowed Charlie at her. "That's my whole point, isn't it? I want you to go with me to Yucatán."

Sheer surprise kept her in her chair, although common sense told her to get up and leave before they disgraced themselves with a scene and were thrown out. As if to remedy her problem, the strolling mariachi band came over to their table, planted themselves at Andy's elbow and burst into a full-blown, full-volume rendition of "Take My Heart." She searched for a mature way to refuse Charlie.

Well, Charlie would take her heart with him, but her body and brain were already spoken for. The Yucatán wasn't for her, she shouted over the chorus. The bandleader's large, melancholy dark eyes became sadder, more liquid, as if she were rejecting him personally.

"Without you," warbled the tenor, "I have no use for it. Take, take, take my heart!"

"I have six weeks more of my classes," she reminded him. "The one I'm teaching, the two that I'm taking. You need a bird of passage, like yourself, content to roam continuously and land briefly, as a companion."

"Don't tell me what *I* need," bellowed Charlie when there was no sign of letup from the serenade. "I asked you. What do you need? You're plugging away on that doctorate just to wangle a permanent teaching job, not because you love petroleum studies. You love me!"

Three male voices joined and blended into a solid wall of sound she could not penetrate. "Listen to the cry it makes with every beat. Take, take, take my heart."

"Let's take, take, take a powder," screeched Andy across the table. Unfortunately the song ended mid-sentence and her loud plea filled the room, attracting the stares and whispers of the other diners. She felt herself getting bright red, unbearably warm, and croaked, "Charlie, let's go, please."

She stood up too quickly, upsetting the basket of rolls, leaving them to bounce on the brick floor. Charlie dropped an uncounted wad of pesos on the table and dashed after her through the courtyard. In the street, she slowed and finally stopped against a rough adobe wall, shadowed and cool.

When Charlie caught up to her, she was more in control of herself. "I don't see why we have to spoil our last night together," she pleaded quietly. "We've been over this ground before, darling. I'm building a nest for myself in San Diego, stick by stick. I worry about my plants on the windowsill when I'm gone. I think about my old age without tenure or pension. How can I just leave and go to Yucatán?"

"It's your life," Charlie said. "You're in charge and make the decisions."

She had a life, a good one, before she met Charlie. It wasn't as sweet or exciting or crazy, that's all. As they walked, aimlessly and slowly, through La Paz, Andy explained what they both already knew. She was going back to school and her apartment, not traipsing after him through jungles or climbing the Pyramids of the Sun.

They wandered to a railing near the docks. The sound and smell of the ocean was reminiscent of other nights, happier ones. The soft lapping of water on the hulls of boats and the pastel glow from the strings of lights decorating the vessels were peaceful and soothing. They spoke in hushed tones, although no one else strolled by to overhear, afraid of disturbing the fragile beauty of the night.

"Then what do I mean to you?" asked Charlie. "What does love mean?"

"You mean a great deal," she answered, fighting the welling of tears. "But you can't mean everything or I'd have nothing else but you. And love . . . love has been like frosting on the cake. I can't thrive on it but I'm glad I tasted it this once."

"You are a tough woman," sighed Charlie. He crossed his arms on the metal bar and hung over it, watching the dark waters work ceaselessly at the pier. "I'm a difficult man, I know, but what if we got married, Andy?"

"It wouldn't change a thing," she said quickly. "Marriage is not a solution, a necessity or a job, as far as I'm concerned. Men seem to think all women are fixated on marriage. I'm not!" She glanced at him. He was not looking at her; he was only thinking aloud, playing with ideas. She fought down a sharp twinge of anger and hurt.

After all these weeks, she thought bitterly, he still doesn't know me. He can't get it through his head that a woman doesn't necessarily want to be taken along with a man. She wanted her own identity and goals to be as important as his; she wouldn't trade her dream for his. Charlie seemed to read her mind, holding her tightly to his side and to the cold metal bar, with an arm around her back, not allowing her to move on.

"I didn't handle that very well," he said. "As a proposal, it wasn't much. I was talking off the top of my head. I'm sorry about spoiling tonight."

His contrition and sincerity won her over. It was easy to get mad at him and hard to stay that way. Andy nestled her head down into his shoulder where it met his neck.

"That's okay, Charlie. Let's go walk on the beach for a while. I want to get my fill of sand between my toes. And then we can go back to the hotel."

"To get your fill of me?" he asked softly.

She closed her eyes. Another night would not be enough no matter how long or closely they clung together. She could foresee her future, searching the dark skies of memory and seeing the brightness and happiness that Charlie had shared with her. But the trail of the comet would eventually fade in time and disappear, and the unpredictable, erratic Charlie Wilde would not come back into her view again.

She didn't answer and Charlie did not press her. They walked on, largely in silence, touching and holding each other to communicate. There was great eloquence in the way Charlie stroked the length of her arms and held her.

The horizon above the Gulf waters was paling to pearl gray and yet they were still on foot, not locked in a parting embrace, a final lovemaking. A few fishermen began to shuffle past them, signaling another day for the real world.

"We can keep walking," Andy said, pausing to slip her sandals back on, "but sooner or later, the sun will come up."

"And you'll be on the plane," Charlie added with a curt nod. "I know. I don't want to have to handle saying goodbye, not good night."

"We don't have to say anything," promised Andy.

She would have preferred silence, a quiet that did not admit that this was, very likely, the last time they would ever make love. It was enough to see sadness in Charlie's eyes and feel desperation as well as passion in his touch.

He undressed her so slowly, it seemed to take forever. Andy felt the hurry of her heart, the intensity of need begin, but she knew why he wouldn't hurry. With every pause to run his fingertips over her skin, Charlie was mapping her for his memory, reasserting a claim on her heart as well as her body. Tonight was all they had left to share.

When she was naked before him, he knelt down and pressed his cheek against the pearly translucent skin of her stomach. The heat of his mouth was like a desert wind.

"You're mine," he said softly, "and I'm yours. I don't want you to forget me."

She held his head tightly to her. "Never," she whispered. It was the truth, as unadorned as she was, as searing as the desire he roused in her. Her thighs parted for his mouth to take intimate possession of her, the stroke of his tongue making her weak, speechless.

She would remember everything. How could she forget how it felt to be loved? However they made love, it was right. Whenever he was joined to her, she felt complete.

She could never forget one moment they'd spent together, spangled in the pure white light of day, or the many nights washed in the thin blue moonlight. She could not ever lose the memory of Charlie's body entering hers, a fierce and consuming pleasure, while his face was filled with love, his eyes adoring.

He held her motionless on the bed beneath himself, trying to prolong their joy. His lips formed the three words that linked them as strongly as their flesh. "I love you."

"I love you, Charlie. Oh, so much...."

There was no way to hold back the dawn or this day. There was no need for more words or the postponement of fulfillment. Afterward, they held each other in silence, legs tangled, arms twined.

When it was time to dress and leave for the airport, Andy got up and simply left. She and Charlie had agreed they could do any number of things to drag out their parting that would only make it more painful. He was outward bound once more; she was homeward bound. She went with rolls and rolls of film, a terrific tan, and George Polachek to drone happily in her ear during the cab ride and on the plane.

The real souvenirs were not packed in her luggage, though. In her head, she heard echoes of voices: the sounds of men talking, the laughs and boasts, and Charlie's whispers in the dark. She saw not clouds and ocean through the plane's narrow window, but a lone heron standing in a mangrove cove and a sky with finely set stars that was more brilliant than the most superb piece of jewelry.

"A solid month to get there and three hours later, I'll be sitting in my chair at home," babbled George. "Hard to believe, isn't it?"

"Uh-huh," said Andy absently. "Like a dream. Just like a dream." She was totally unprepared, thoroughly baffled when the tears began to fall and a storm of sobs shook her.

Eleven

Pacific Polytechnic's library was nearly deserted when Andromeda arrived. There was less than a hour left before the official closing of the building. She scurried past two dedicated students, cramming for exams while stuffing their faces with strictly prohibited foods. She pretended not to see them because to see meant she should duly report them to MacIver, the chief keeper of knowledge. She had no intention of squealing; she herself was smuggling in a sandwich and a white paper cup of coffee.

"Oh, a word with you, Ms. Pruitt!" someone called to her back, and Andy jumped a foot off the slick tile floor. She managed a sickly smile when Dr. Findlay, head of her department, rushed up and took her elbow. "You are a difficult woman to reach," he intoned.

The cup she was balancing inside the confines of a baggy

cardigan sweater tipped when he tugged on her arm. Andy felt a trickle of hot liquid creep down her side.

If his reputation was based on fact, Dr. Findlay was able to breathe fire and devour young knights and maidens.

"I got your messages," she explained rapidly, trying not to wince with pain. "I really meant to get back to you, Dr. Findlay, but I've had to catch up on so many things since my vacation...student appointments, papers, making some research studies for Waverly... Now I didn't miss a single class but I'm behind on everything else."

The older, distinguished man ordered, "Please, Ms. Pruitt, put a sock in it, will you? My faculty are worse than students. I'm not dropping the ax on you." He gave her a smile that sent undergraduates into fits of stark terror. "Quite the contrary. I wanted you to come and discuss the possibility of more teaching for the next term."

"Really?" Andy blurted out. She felt more coffee slosh along her. "I mean, how very nice. But, Dr. Findlay, there's a problem with full-time teaching and me. You see, I must have some evenings free for my astronomy and—"

"Full time is out of the question," interrupted Findlay, relieving her and deflating Andy's ego at the same time. "You're very popular with the students and they have demonstrated an acceptable level of learning from your class, but you do not have a Ph.D., Ms. Pruitt. We simply can't consider more than two or three classes for you until you obtain your credentials. Call my secretary and come in when you're available."

He was plainly finished with her before Andy got her chance to speak. "Salary?" she asked loudly as he turned. "Labs? Hours?"

"I hear *Sky and Telescope* is buying an article from you," he said, dismissing her questions with a frown. "You mustn't expect a raise for part-time work, and we may expect, I'm sure, you will want to take off if anything marvelous appears on the horizon."

"I'll call and set up an appointment," Andy yelled after him. She was pleased with the offer but part of her wished she could tell Findlay to fly a kite. She was at the bottom of his academic totem pole and he wanted her to know it.

"Working after hours tonight?" MacIver's friendlier voice drifted out of his open office.

Andy nodded and used a small chat with the librarian to restore her good humor. The cartography section of the building was too small, too crowded with students for her purposes during most days. Andy had her key to the library for this late research, a peanut butter and jelly feast for dinner and a very wet blouse. MacIver escorted Andy down to the area set aside for maps, surveys and aerial photographs. She studiously avoided looking down at the tan trail of drips she was leaving on his nice white tiles.

"As soon as I shoo everyone else out," Mac promised in a conspiratorial whisper, "I'll bring you a piece of my birthday cake. A cup of tea, too, if you like. And a sponge mop."

"Ah, dessert," giggled Andy. "Okay, Mac."

It was the first laugh she'd had in too long. Since her return from La Paz, Andy knew she was driving herself too hard. Her juggling act included more than her duties on campus and the wedging-in of hours for her hobby. She'd come back unsure of what and where the teaching would lead, and started in on preliminary reports for Waverly Oil. She had to keep all her opportunities moving, like small brightly colored balls in the air.

It was better to stay busy and do the things she liked to do best, pre-Charlie, than to leave herself free to remember too much. She hadn't told anyone about the trip in any detail; there weren't many people, she realized, that she was close to.

There were colleagues like Mac to talk with and students to teach. There were men like Dr. Findlay to deal with. But there was no one to laugh or cry with, no one to tease and kid unmercifully. Before she loved Charles Wilde, Andy was not bothered by the lack of a special man in her life.

She was now. She flipped idly through the files, restless and unable to settle down to work. The utter silence and solitude of the cartography room made her uneasy. She found a huge map of the Yucatán and slid it out of the pile to study until she admitted her interest was not in locating Chichén Itzá. Where was Charlie? Was he happy?

Almost angrily, Andy pushed the map back into place. She'd get more work done once she convinced herself that Wilde was busy, pointing out highlights of archaeological sites to a captivated, curvy redhead. She'd make money if all her speculations were centered on Waverly Oil prospects and not on her own future, alone.

Poring over a minutely detailed survey of Wyoming, she lost herself in the hunt for new green pastures of energy. The whisper of pencils taking notes and the occasional ticking sounds from the fluorescent lights above were the only sounds until a hideous noise split through the library and shattered her peace.

She raised her head, recognizing the unique timbre of the man's shout. "Someone let a bear loose in church," Andy said to herself and got up from the table. Her name reverberated in the library, echoed down the halls. Few people were named Andromeda.

There was a scuffling in the corridor and the indistinct arguments of Mac, violently protesting. The clomping of heavy boots drowned out most of Mac's words but she had already got the message. Speak of the Devil, and he will appear.

"Hi, Charlie," Andy said when he arrived and stopped at the doorway. "Long time, no see...and similar sentiments."

"A month," bellowed Charlie. He shook Mac off his arm like a dry leaf. "Pruitt, call this guy off, will you?"

"I'll ring the campus police," Mac announced, plucking ineffectively at a grimy khaki sleeve of Charlie's shirt. "You can't just bust into my library, Mr...."

"It's okay, Mac," Andy said a bit weakly. "Let him stay."

Charlie looked wonderful to her but, objectively, he resembled a zoo escapee. His beard was back in full force. His face was tanned to deepest mahogany, matching his glittering eyes. He was an imposing, impressive and distinctly scary figure. Yet seeing him, she felt as though the sun had just risen in the middle of the night.

"See?" Charlie was saying to the perplexed librarian. "Everything's cool. I'm fine. I'm here to see Andromeda, not to steal books."

MacIver glanced up and down Charlie and back to Andy, justifiably dubious. "Do you want me to stay close by?"

"He's Wilde but not dangerous," said Andy with a smile. "If he doesn't behave himself, I'll throw a map over his head and bean him with a globe."

"Let the punishment fit the crime," Charlie shot back at her. "I can see the headlines now. 'World Traveler Meets Well Deserved Fate.'"

MacIver obviously had no idea of what was happening, but he was partially pacified by their laughter. He rubbed his balding crown and slouched off, thoroughly confused.

Andy's only confusion was what to do first: tell Charlie how much she missed him in four weeks or show him. Her dilemma was resolved easily. Charlie came barreling over to her, lifting her off the floor and smothering her with his hairy, enthusiastic kiss. His beard tickled and scratched, but she didn't object. No man could kiss better than Charlie Wilde, she was convinced. He put his heart, his soul and all the time they'd missed together into it.

"Air! Air!" she wheezed into his mouth, wondering whether she would faint from excitement or his incredibly tight grip.

"I'll shave," replied Charlie, pulling his leonine head back fractionally. "Damn, Pruitt, I would have shaved but I came looking for you straight from the airport."

"Air, not hair," she explained. Her fingers dug in the thickness of his mane and scratched his chin with delight. "Set me down, Charlie. I can't feel my toes; they've gone numb. This position is both undignified and uncomfortable."

He complied in his own fashion, putting her on the outspread map covering the table. With his weight on her and his elbows resting on either side of her, she was his willing prisoner. "Glad to see me?" He beamed down at her, knowing the answer.

She laughed, her head falling back and leaving her throat bare and vulnerable to an attack of kisses, nibbles. Charlie made muffled and appreciative sounds. Andy had to tug on his ears to make him stop.

"Yes," she whispered, drinking in the sight of him. "Yes, I'm glad. Life is certainly a good deal duller without you. I've had lots more time to sit and stare out into space, Charlie, but I'm enjoying it less."

"Lots less, hopefully." He touched her cheek as if he needed to assure himself of her reality. "I couldn't wait to be finished in Yucatán. The tour went well and I made some money. The group was real nice and cooperative but . . ."

"Boring?" she inserted, and he nodded yes. "I thought it was just me," she went on. "You must have had some thrills in the jungles."

"This trip wasn't the same," Charlie said softly, "because getting away from it all included being away from you this time. I didn't like it, Andy. I love what I do but I love you, too. I spent every hot, humid night—alone, incidentally—figuring out how a man can have everything."

She tried to lever herself up from under him and failed. Her hand flew to his mouth, blocking his words, while her memory flashed back to a beach in La Paz. "We can't have everything, remember? Charlie, I love you. I adore you, in fact. But, a month ago in Mexico, we agreed neither one of us would give up our lives for our love. I haven't come up with a solution in a month."

"I have," Charlie said with a wicked gleam in his eye. "You want someone you can count on, someone who's there for you, but you want to live as an independent, productive woman, too."

"Right," she said. "I don't want a bird of passage who is flitting here and there while I'm stuck teaching and getting my Ph.D. I'm not a part-time woman."

"You'd be happier some place there was a good, cloudless sky," contradicted Charlie. "You aren't even set on teaching, Andromeda. You'd just do anything that gave you a couple nights a week to roam in outer space."

"A person has to eat, Charlie," she snapped and pinched him to make him jump. "A woman should be able to buy her own panty hose."

"You could work with me," he said quickly, running his words together. "We'd take twice as many people, yes, men and women, on every Wilde tour... South America in two months. I see advertising special lectures given by you on geography, earth science and astronomy... we'd pack 'em in...."

"What?" She realized an old feeling was overtaking her. They were fighting again while fooling around. Charlie's hands were roaming her body, loosening her damp blouse from the waistband of the jeans. She slapped at the back of his hand. "You are insane!"

"Ladies and gents, our tours are educational," he proclaimed in ringing tones to the acoustic ceiling. His fingers stroked her bare ribs and gave her goose bumps. "Action-filled! Wilde 'N Free builds sound minds *and* healthy bodies!"

"Not with me," shrieked Andy, wriggling violently. She lowered her voice, dreading MacIver would appear any second and assume she was being raped on his sacred library tables. "Why on earth would I want to become a Gypsy?"

"You have a reasonably sound mind and an amazingly healthy body to preserve," Charlie said. "But mostly, you love me. We'd be together morning, noon and you'd have every night off, if you wanted it. You could be my *partner*!" He made it sound like a title any executive would kill for.

"No home," muttered Andy under her breath. "No pension, no tenure, no..."

"Me and you, Andromeda Wilde," Charlie pronounced the last syllable very carefully and with heavy emphasis. "It would be a very fitting, appropriate name. It has a nice ring to it." He grinned at her before his head swooped back into hiding in her neck. "Nice ring," his deep voice repeated "Get it? That's a pun."

"That's a real proposal," Andy clarified, feeling light-headed. Her dizzy state returned and it seemed to have less to do with an offer of marriage than with the havoc Charlie's kisses were wreaking with her nervous system. A few more minutes of Wilde persuasion and she wouldn't care who waltzed through the door and caught them.

"Let me up," she whispered urgently to him. "I'm creasing this map, Charlie, and you are messing up my mind."

He complied but kept her in his embrace, tucked securely between his legs and held in his arms. He stroked her hair, letting the fine strands slide through his fingers like the golden sands of the Gulf. "I'm glad I still have some effect on you. Driving over here, I was worried. What if you'd forgotten me? What if you didn't want to remember me or the trip or the Baja?"

"Highly unlikely," Andy said with a faint smile. "You are a memorable man, to put it mildly."

"And I didn't stop thinking about you, Andy. Not for a minute, not for a second since we said goodbye. You can ask me anything about the Yucatán and I'll make up a story because I wasn't completely there most of the time. Physically, yes, but I kept thinking..."

"About me?"

When he stopped talking and his eyes grew darker but curiously brighter, she knew he wanted to make love to her. She could not make sense of this reunion or decide what to do about loving him.

Andy pulled one of her arms free and ran her hand upward to rest on Charlie's chest. She meant to push him away ever so slightly and give herself a little space, a little dis-

ance. Under her widespread fingers, she felt his heart
beating; it was a rapid rhythm—excited or fearful.

Was he afraid his solution wouldn't work? He'd known
the failure of a marriage and she hadn't. Or, worse, was
Charlie afraid she would accept? He never had much hope
for the institution of marriage, as she recalled. He wanted
her with him, but marriage was a permanent state, not a
place to visit.

"It's too stuffy in here," Charlie said. "You know I don't
do well in confined spaces. Come outside, Andy, and I'll
make more sense."

"You should meet Dr. Findlay, my boss," complained
Andy. "Talk about stuffy."

She went out with him onto the wide steps of the library
and they stood there, both of them temporarily silenced by
the unexpected glory of the sunset's purples and pinks.
Charlie's red Jeep was carelessly parked too close to the entrance, and a ticket fluttered in the gentle breeze from under the windshield wiper.

"Caught in the snares of civilization," said Andy, gesturing at the paper. "You can't settle down, Charlie. Marriage is too settled, too civilized for a man like you. You
haven't been back for more than a couple of hours and
you're already in trouble with the law. How are you and I
going to coexist peacefully for years?"

"We won't," said Charlie flatly. He thrust his hands deep
into his pockets and took a tentative sniff of the evening
winds. "We'll do what we did for a thousand miles of the
Baja. We'll scrap and quarrel and drive each other crazy."

"Oh, that sounds enticing," Andy said sarcastically. "My
stars, no one can say you don't speak the truth, either."

"We'll also make up and make love," Charlie went on,
ignoring her comment. "We do those things exceptionally

well, too. We have more fun together than any two people
can think of and we are the most evenly matched couple in
the entire world. That's the truth, isn't it, Andromeda
Wilde?''

"If I took you, I wouldn't take your name," Andy heard
herself say without thinking. "Someday I have the intention of discovering a fabulous Pruitt comet, not a Wilde
one."

Charlie turned toward her and gave her a bear hug, dragging her down the steps with him toward the Jeep. "I think
you're too late, darling. Here we are, a two-headed wonder
of a comet. We're both racing around in our own orbit, not
caring how strange we appear to observers. But, okay, if you
need your own identity, you'll stay Pruitt. Our business
stays Wilde Tours."

"I did not say yes," Andy remarked, climbing in without a murmur. "I'm considering Dr. Findlay's latest offer
of a fine teaching career."

Charlie scratched the bridge of his nose meditatively.
"Don't count on Doc Findlay," he said. "I went to your
office looking for you before I hit the library. It was, I believe, your department chairman who directed me after I
kicked up a fuss on his doorstep. Short, stubborn little
cuss."

"Charlie?" She rolled her eyes at him and grimaced.
"Dare I ask what you did? Am I linked forever in his mind
with an escaped lunatic?"

"In answer to the first question, you don't want to know
the gory details," he replied placidly. "In answer to the
second, yes."

She didn't need details; she could see an enraged, insistent Charlie towering over the dapper, ultraconservative
Findlay. If there was a rank below the base of the totem

pole, she would find a shovel in her mailbox tomorrow morning. Some groveling and countless assurances that she did not regularly associate with such bizarre, unprofessional men would suffice—but she wasn't going to grovel or beg.

A long peal of laughter erupted from her throat. "Did Findlay give you much trouble, Charlie?"

"Not as much as you do."

She began thinking about South America, days and days boating along the Orinoco River and nights in Charlie's arms. Well, there were bound to be plenty of cloudy nights, rainy nights when she couldn't use the telescope.

"How about Pruitt-Wilde, with a hyphen?" He moved over, adjusting himself around the gearshift to close in on her. He began to kiss her earlobe, moist and warm kisses like a rain forest.

"There is no hyphen between us. Charlie, there are laws about this kind of activity in public. In a second, there will be nothing between us."

She felt one button after another open down the front of her blouse. A gently possessive hand slipped in to reclaim territory he knew very well. With a light brush of his thumb, Charlie was capable of raising a peak to rival an Andean mountain on her breast.

He was skillfully and successfully maneuvering her with his tall frame into the door of the Jeep. Her ability to protest was hampered by his mouth, pressed firmly to hers, and by her own soaring enjoyment of everything he was doing. Andy's eyes rolled frantically around the darkening campus and saw, thankfully, not a soul.

"We have everything between us...before us," whispered Charlie, lifting his head finally. "Andromeda, if any two humans were made for each other, it's you and me."

"Who else would have us?" she feebly joked.

The tip of his tongue flicked out and traced a path from her collarbone to one round, pale breast, circling the nipple. When he spoke, the words made her whole body vibrate and sent long, chilly sensations down her spine. "See what I mean? We can disagree even while we're agreeing on a very basic and important level."

Andy touched him and found ample evidence that they were, indeed, getting down to basics. Charlie groaned and unsnapped the button on her jeans, putting his mouth on the satiny skin he exposed.

"You are a beast," Andy said happily. "Not here, Charlie."

"You are an angel," he responded instantly. "Where?"

"Where what?" she asked a few minutes later when she realized he was not talking any more. "Where are we going to spend the night?"

"You are an angel," he repeated impatiently and heaved some of his weight off her, "and I love you more than heaven itself, but, sometimes, you act dense…dear. Where are we going to get married?"

Andy arranged her arms around his neck and nuzzled his face. "I'll need time to think about marriage, Wilde. I want to make absolutely sure it's the best move for me."

"Take all the time you want or need," Charlie said with an expansive gesture. "You can give me your answer in the morning."

"No! You know how mellow and muddled I am early in the mornings."

"Next weekend, when you hike with me in the San Gabriel wilderness?"

"No! Right now I have a commitment to a real job."

He sighed, sat up and ran his fingers madly through his bushy hair until it stood up straight all around his head. "What an impossible... By the time we leave for South America we'll be married. All right?"

"Maybe," Andy allowed, falling onto his shoulder. She attempted to smooth down his hair and failed. He was wild and woolly, but she couldn't imagine loving another man but Charlie. He wouldn't change most of his ways that drove her batty but then he wouldn't want her to change to suit him in return.

"I love you," Charlie said for the third time that night. "I'll take you to Africa next year, Andromeda, and you'll see meteor showers that'll knock your eyes out. I don't want a part-time woman or marriage. I want you and I need you always."

She bit her lip and held back the tears that came, suddenly and unbidden, to her eyes. There was no doubting the sincerity of Charlie's love. She envisioned the stability and security he was offering in simply being with him, getting up and going to sleep with him from today on and forever. They were like comets, perhaps, but they could also be like the sun to each other: giving heat and fire, lighting up the rest of their lives.

"Africa," she said in wonder. "Probably Alaska and the Arctic Circle next. I could really do justice to photographing the northern lights."

Charlie started up the engine, nudging her slightly back to the passenger side. "Glad we got it settled," he sighed. "I'm tired of chasing you all over town. Let's go to your apartment. My office isn't in any better shape than the last time you saw it."

"By 2061, there will be a Pruitt-Wilde watching for Halley's Comet," said Andy dreamily, more to herself than to him. "Charlie, by then, there will probably be a shuttle flight to take our children up for a closer look."

"I'll be a hundred and ten and we'll both be rafting down the Colorado River," Charlie said confidently.

She dissolved into helpless laughter and banged on the side of the Jeep appreciatively. The stars overhead blinked at her as if they were approving and signaling to her. He was a strange and wonderful man.

Sometime she would have to tell him that she had known all along that there was no point in catching a comet. If a comet was intercepted or knocked off its own course, it would be destroyed. The best thing anyone could do was to find a comet and travel along with it until the end of time.

"Yes, Charlie" was all she could manage to say, but he understood. His hand closed over hers and held on.

 # Silhouette Desire

COMING NEXT MONTH

LOVEPLAY—Diana Palmer
When Edward McCullough set out to write his new play, he never intended for his old flame, Bett, to act in his cast. But Bett was determined to convince him that their love was still in the script.

FIRESTORM—Doreen Owens Malek
Jason was haunted by the accident that had left him widowed. But then he met Alison, his son's teacher, who taught him not to let the darkness in his past color their chance for a bright future.

JULIET—Ashley Summers
Determined to rebuild her family's fortune, Juliet was going to need some help. Cord was a Romeo in disguise. But could he save her from ruin and win her for himself?

SECRET LOVE—Nancy John
By day they were enemies, rival experts for the world's two most famous auction houses. But by night, Paula and Quinn savored a love that knew no allegiances.

FOOLISH PLEASURE—Jennifer Greene
Passion still flared between Stephanie and Alex long after their divorce—and their son was bent on playing matchmaker. Steph wasn't going to get close to Alex again, but how could she deny an undeniable love?

TEXAS GOLD—Joan Hohl
When model Barbara Holcomb arrived to assist her elderly aunt, she found herself in the midst of a real Texan manhunt. Her partner in pursuit was Ranger Thackery Sharp, but it was soon unclear who was pursuing whom!

Take 4 Silhouette Intimate Moments novels FREE

Then preview 4 brand new Silhouette Intimate Moments® novels —delivered to your door every month—for 15 days as soon as they are published. When you decide to keep them, you pay just $2.25 each ($2.50 each, in Canada), *with no shipping, handling, or other charges of any kind!*

Silhouette Intimate Moments novels are not for everyone. They were created to give you a more detailed, more exciting reading experience, filled with romantic fantasy, intense sensuality, and stirring passion.

The first 4 Silhouette Intimate Moments novels are absolutely FREE and without obligation, yours to keep. You can cancel at any time.

You'll also receive a FREE subscription to the Silhouette Books Newsletter as long as you remain a member. Each issue is filled with news on upcoming titles, interviews with your favorite authors, even their favorite recipes.

To get your 4 FREE books, fill out and mail the coupon today!

Silhouette Intimate Moments®

Silhouette Books, 120 Brighton Rd., P.O. Box 5084, Clifton, NJ 07015-5084

READERS' COMMENTS ON SILHOUETTE DESIRES

"Thank you for Silhouette Desires. They are the best thing that has happened to the bookshelves in a long time."
—V.W.*, Knoxville, TN

"Silhouette Desires—wonderful, fantastic—the best romance around."
—H.T.*, Margate, N.J.

"As a writer as well as a reader of romantic fiction, I found DESIREs most refreshingly realistic—and definitely as magical as the love captured on their pages."
—C.M.*, Silver Lake, N.Y.

"I just wanted to let you know how very much I enjoy your Silhouette Desire books. I read other romances, and I must say your books rate up at the top of the list."
—C.N.*, Anaheim, CA

"Desires are number one. I especially enjoy the endings because they just don't leave you with a kiss or embrace; they finish the story. Thank you for giving me such reading pleasure."
—M.S.*, Sandford, FL

*names available on request